Patrick McStup's Mixed-Up Family

CHRISTMAS part 1

THE MCERLEAN BROTHERS
Written by Patrick • Illustrated by Michael

gatekeeper press
Columbus, Ohio

To Brandy, Kylee, Avery, & my entire family

Patrick McStup's Mixed-Up Family Christmas part 1

Published by Gatekeeper Press
2167 Stringtown Rd, Suite 109
Columbus, OH 43123-2989
www.GatekeeperPress.com

First Edition

Written by: Patrick McErlean

Cover design/art, Book design, & Illustrations by: Michael McErlean

Additional Illustrations by: Patrick McErlean, Wil McErlean, Kylee McErlean, & Avery McErlean

Edited and/or Proofread by: Mike Viso, Jim Johansen, Michael McErlean, Brandy McErlean, & Mona Mistric

ISBN (hardcover): 9781642377781
ISBN (paperback): 9781642377798
eISBN: 9781642377804

Library of Congress Control Number: 2019951093

www.themcstupfamily.com

ACKNOWLEDGEMENTS

First, I'd like to thank God! I truly believe God helped guide me through this challenging journey and gave me the confidence and vision to make all of this become a reality!

I would like to thank each and every one of my family members, who made this dream a reality—from my beautiful wife, Brandy, and our wonderful daughters, Kylee and Avery; to my Dad and Mom; as well as all of my brothers and sisters! Over the years I have written down notebooks full of anything that struck me as funny, quirky, or not the typical things all of us would normally say or do. If it wasn't for my crazy, fun-loving family, there wouldn't be any stories for me to tell. Thank you again for being who you are and thank you for inspiring me to write these stories!

A BIG thank you to my brother, Mike, who spent countless hours illustrating everything as well as helping me fine-tune the entire story. This story definitely would not be the same without his input!!

Special thanks to:

Wil, Kylee, and Avery McErlean for additional illustrations.

Jimmy & Brandy McErlean for feedback.

Laura Davis, Dave Meyers, and Mike Smick for taking the time to help us with any questions we had about the business.

Thank you to all of the editors and proofreaders who supported me: Mike Viso, Jim Johansen, Michael McErlean, Brandy McErlean, and Mona Mistric.

And, thank you to everyone who will take the time to read these stories. I hope this brings laughter, happiness and joy to all!

THE DRAFT

Sorry to all you Christmas "lovers" out there, BUT I think I love Christmas more than anybody on this whole dang planet Earth!

Go ahead and say I'm obsessed with Christmas because I am obsessed with Christmas. I eat, sleep, drink, and dream about it all the time.

In fact, if I had only one Christmas wish—ONLY ONE WISH—my wish would be to visit the pole of poles—THE NORTH POLE!!

Can you imagine...being knocked out by Santa, so you can't see what route he takes to get you to the North Pole!

I'm pretty darn positive he would fly me right into the side of a mountain!

It would be the side that has one of those waterfalls that is secretly disguised as a cave—the Santa cave!

Then, as the formaldehyde or whatever chemical Santa used to knock me out with wears off, I slowly wake up and BOOM! I'm at the North Pole!

A place that only a handful of humans have ever visited!

I heard that almost everything up there is edible. That's right, you can eat anything from the grass to the wallpaper; and SHOOT, I heard you can even have yourself a snow cone made from yellow snow!

I'd find me a reindeer and ride it like it's never been rode before! It should be easier than riding a horse because I think I can use the antlers as handlebars or a steering wheel.

I'd get to interview Mrs. Clause and find out exactly just what it is that makes her tick. Maybe I'd ask her some awkward questions like: How old are you? What is your dress size? Where did you and Santa go on your honeymoon? What did you guys do while you were on your honeymoon? Do you have any kids? If so, why the heck do we never hear anything about them? What are your current sugar levels? I have so many questions!

And as for Santa, well, I would probably be so starstruck that I wouldn't be able to do anything but stare at him for THE ENTIRE TIME! No matter what he would talk to me about, I would probably just stare at him.

Also, and this is very important, I'd have to touch him.

I have a little bit of obsessive-compulsive disorder (OCD), so I would have to do this! I mean, what the heck is the point of meeting someone if you can't even touch him or her, right?

Also, I'd HAVE to bring back a souvenir...something that when people see it, they would know, undoubtedly, that I did indeed go to the North Pole. That way, everyone would know I'd become chummy with Santa and his wifey.

I know what I should do! I'd go after his beard! I would put a few rubber bands here and there into his beard like bikers do, so they can contain it.

Then, I would just snip it off right under his chin. Hopefully, he would be cool with that and give me a jolly old laugh!

It can't get much better than that!

Ahhhh, I'm on this Christmas high note right now and nobody can bring me down from it, at least not for the next few hours.

That's when we go and pick up my archenemy, Grandma Bertha, who will be staying with us for a few days. (A Moment of silence)

Side note: Grandma Bertha and I do NOT get along at ALL! In fact, she was voted the #2 super villain of ALL TIME on my ALL TIME Super Villain list! Congrats to Grandma Bertha for doing the unthinkable. She somehow literally leapfrogged my sinister sister, Petunia, to take that #2 spot.

Who is my #1 super villain of all time? THAT, I am saving for another time and another story!

Grandma Bertha's stinking up our house for the next few days is not great news at all. And, to make things worse...I may or may not have to go shopping with my Dad...who's kind of nuts!

I'm not worrying about it though because I may not even have to go shopping at all. However, the possibility is kind of real, so I'm just waiting to see how things play out.

Right now...is the worst time to go shopping!

Reasons why you ask?

A) We have procrastinated for days, and we have SO much food to get for Christmas dinner.

B) Stuff always happens when we go shopping. It's never just a get in and get out peaceful kind of experience.

C) DAD HATES GOING SHOPPING, and we all have to listen to it! He hates going shopping on Saturdays because EVERYONE who is off work is going shopping on that day. AND, he hates shopping around the holidays because the stores are what he calls "mad houses".

Today is a Saturday AND it's Christmas Eve. What a combination, just GREAT!

Wow! There is so much to do, so before any of us leave the house we must conjure up a game plan. The idea is to divide us up between our Mom and our Dad.

Some of us will stay home to help Mom straighten up the house, and some of us will go to the store to help Dad with the shopping. But, who stays and who goes?

Usually, I would want to stay home and avoid this headache. BUT, if I go, I just might get a sneak preview of a potential BIG last-minute gift with my name on it!

Just to let everyone know, as of this morning, I have been extremely good. I've been trying to show my parents AND Santa my new and improved self in hopes of having them upgrade any or all of my presents.

Plus, the house is in extra horrible condition, so I'd rather all the SUCKERS (brothers and sisters) stay and clean up this mess! Don't tell Santa I said that.

In the meantime, a few of us brothers and sisters are looking over our BIG Christmas catalog. Petunia is always looking at these catalogs. She is always mumbling how all she wants for Christmas is to look like this model, or that model, or the model on the next page when she grows up. I think it's because they wear these nice clothes and have all this makeup all over their faces.

Turning page by page, we put our names next to any item that we like. We sit and wonder if it's at all possible that we would get any of those amazing things.

Petunia is the one turning the pages now and seems most anxious with how many times I put my name next to an item. She calls it "ridiculous" and "so unrealistic."

She says, "You're always trying to pretend you're a man; however, would a MAN circle over 700 items in a Christmas catalog—TOY section?" I glare at her to avoid any arguments.

Petunia smirks, "Just for the heck of it, I sat down a few days ago with a calculator and added up all of the items with your name next to them. Just take a guess how much the total was for all those items you circled?"

I replied in my most manly voice, "What is this, a game show? Petunia's 'I have no life, so I'm going to add up all of the things that my awesome brother circled in the Christmas catalog game?'"

I tell her, "I have no idea, BUT if I have to take a wild guess, I would say it has to be a little more than $175."

It's nice to see Petunia laugh because her laugh makes me laugh. When she laughs hysterically, it turns into an ugly uncalled for laugh that only scientists can understand and that's after they have studied it for years.

Chills me to the bone.

I tell her, "A man can dream, right?"

After she calms down and is able to breathe, she informs me that I'm not even close. Petunia says, "$175, what a horrible guess. I know I'll never choose you as a partner on any game show, that's for sure. Your grand total, when you add up everything that you circled, comes out to be exactly: TWO HUNDRED..." (I interrupt her and tell her that is a lot closer than what she is giving me credit for!)

After a brief pause, she continues..."TWO HUNDRED THOUSAND, FIVE HUNDRED SEVENTY NINE DOLLARS!"

I come back with "$200,579...so what? I know that I'm not getting all of that stuff! I would be happy if I only got half of that because..." (She interrupts me and does that hysterical alien laugh again.)

She always laughs or makes fun of me, and I do not like it! I try to silently let her know that I'll be keeping my eyes on her. I do one of those pointing at her with my 2 fingers then I slowly come back and point at my eyes.

I don't know how I did it, but I accidentally poked my own eyes when I came back with my fingers. Of course, that led to even more Petunia laughter!

I think I may have some fiber optic nerve damage in the renal portion/area of my retina due to my finger poke.

As my vision starts coming back towards me, I notice Dad and Mom are sitting, talking and writing down notes about what is going to happen here.

I act all cool about this, as I intently watch Dad and Mom's discussion through the corners of my eyes. I'm lip reading the heck out of the both of them and notice the word "Patrick" is coming up often!

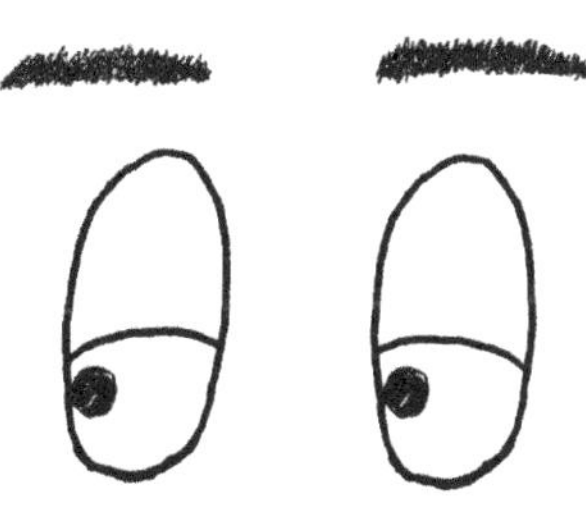

Hmmm, it seems as though they are both fighting over my services. But, let's see who wants me the most. That is the question!

Our parents continue to strategize and choose who will stay and who will go. Some of us don't want to go and some of us don't want to stay.

I don't really care, as I am again, just interested in seeing who chooses me and in what order I am chosen.

And with that said...

With the 1st overall pick in the 'which of us stays home and which of us goes shopping draft', Team Dad selects:

From the University of Burbank High school in Burbank Illinois, A 5'7, 130 lb. HUNK of talent, Patrick McStup!!!!

Side note: It's Patrick McStup! Pronounced like Patrick Mixed-Up, not Patrick Mac-Stup!

My fist is pumping in the air, as I slowly stand. I fix my imaginary suit and tie and I get my baseball hat out as I shake Commissioner Dad's hand!

First and foremost, I'd like to thank God for giving me abilities.

A slight pause occurs, as I bite my lower lip and hold back tears of joy.

Second, I'd like to be traded to team Mom!

I just realized that Grandma Bertha would be on my team and she basically sucks, so I am giving my 2-minute notice. Aaaaand, I'd like to be traded this instant!

Dad denies my request and tells me to sit down. I can't even negotiate this; it's such a helpless feeling.

He better watch it: otherwise, I might become... DISGRUNTLED!

While we're shopping, I could go out there and blatantly fumble every loaf of bread, or squash every single grape on the vine, or I could take off every eggnog cap that enters our shopping cart, but I am bigger than that.

Because it's Christmas, I'll try and get along with Grandma. PLUS, Santa, Dad and Mom will be able to see my good intentions and the hard work that I have been doing while being around Grandma Bertha's big butt!

Maybe Dad will get me a little something extra for Christmas while we are in the store...I don't know, we will see.

So, here's a quick summary of the 'who stays and who goes draft':

Team Mom...BOO!

Team Mom consists of:

Mom (the captain) is a stay at home Mom, who fakes fainting to get us to stop fighting. It's best if you're on her good side! I try not to look directly into her eyes.

Petunia is the oldest sibling and the one God put specifically on this Earth just to test me! She's motherly, average to decent cook, and an after the fact psychic!

Cecil is a younger brother, who loves to fight, yet loves unicorns? He's always starving for attention. Random!

Ernie is another younger brother, who is in his second go around of first grade.

Side note: Ernie also had to repeat kindergarten!

Baby Beulah is NOT a baby, but we call her "Baby Beulah" since she is the youngest.

Side note: I don't know what we would do if Dad and Mom had another baby! That would be way too confusing!

Anyway, Team Mom will stay at home and get the cleaning and cooking and whatever they were going to get done...done! Enough about Team Mom, as the music starts to play...

Next, you have Team Dad. Annnd, the crowd goes BONKERS!

Team Dad consists of:

Dad (the captain) should legally have his name changed to "Mad Dad" because he is always MAD, and he is always DAD!

Patrick is very modest and a gifted athlete! People not only love him but they also flock to him...in pairs. He wants to one day build an ark to save the pairs of people who flock to him. He's a "charmer" and a natural born leader. His nickname is "Stud muffin"! There's a lot more, but he's too modest to tell all. Also, one day, he will be a Superhero!

Luther is another younger brother, who is also Patrick's sidekick, protector and the one who clashes with authority figures, like parents, cops, nuns, teachers, management, etc. He's a Leo, which explains a lot.

Gertrude is a younger sister and supposedly the "Normal" one. She's Dad's favorite, since she's smart and destined to become something great!

Gunther is the youngest brother. He LOVES food, LOVES to play and LOVES to play with his food. He's rather quiet and full of surprises. He can take his foot and kick it over his head!

Grandma Bertha, Bingo Wing Queen herself, will be stinking up the place. If you don't have anything nice to say about someone you should just not say anything at all. So, all I'm saying is that she is stupid and evil!

Side note: Bingo wings are the flabby part of the upper arm that hangs down, the skin that covers the triceps. Grandma has AWESOME bingo wings—hands down. It's my favorite thing about her.

I gather our team up and force them to put their hands out to form a circle. I always wanted to do this: "OK, listen up. On 5 Mississippis, WE DO THIS THING!

"One Mississippi...

"Two Mississippi...

"Three Mississippi...

"Four Mississippi...

"Five Mississippi!"

No participation, except from me, so I make a "Yeeeee Hawwww" noise, but still nothing really happened. I realize this huddle thing is quite stupid and is overrated and really serves no purpose at all.

Luther said he wants to guard Baby Beulah, who is the smallest, so at least one of us finally moves from our awkward circle.

CYBER FRIDAY!

We head out on a short trip to go and get Grandma Bertha, who lives in Chicago! Right before we get to her place, I take a few deep breaths, followed by twenty quick short breaths, followed by some more deep breaths.

While sitting in the car in front of Grandma's apartment, I watch Dad and her slowly walk the non-shoveled sidewalk back towards the car. I can tell that she is in a great mood because she always sings this happy song that doesn't make much sense at all.

♫♪ "DOUGH DIT DE DOUGH–DIT DE DOUGH...
DIT DE DOUGH.
DOUGH DIT DE DOUGH–DIT DE DOUGH...
DIT DE DOUGH.
DOUGH DIT DE DOUGH–DIT DE DOUGH." ♪♫

I've been trying to decipher this code for years. I think it's some Irish jibber-jabber language, but I'm not sure.

I hate when she sings this song because I can't even go a minute without it getting stuck in my head. And the worst part is that it's not even a good song.

Her "Dough dit de dough's" stop when she notices that I'm in the car looking at her.

As she enters the car, she looks at me and gives me a great big sigh, as she blurts out, "YOU? You ruin every single room you're in!" Then she gives me an eye roll.

What's up with that? It's like she has been waiting to say that to me. I'm not even in a room; I'm in a car.

That's just a horrible greeting!

Grandma YELLS at Dad and asks him why he still brought me along AFTER he said he would leave me at home. Dad replies to Grandma by saying, "I had to bring him with. I need his help with the grocery shopping." I then whisper to Grandma, "Do you want me to just open the car door and push you out now, or should I wait until we start moving?"

DAAAAAAARN IT! Christmas is not supposed to be a violent time. It's supposed to be about Jesus' Birthday, Santa, watching that movie on TV that is repeated over and over for 24 hours; and of course, all of my presents that I will be getting!

I realized this wasn't the best way to go about things, so I try to start things off on the left foot by offering Grandma Bertha some "Peacetime".

Side note: Peacetime is when you touch the tip of your nose to someone else's forehead and either spell out the word "p-e-a-c-e", or you draw out the "peace fingers" symbol on their forehead—your choice. Then, they graciously return the Peacetime to you. It just signals a "peaceful" greeting between 2 people. Plus, these days, people just don't want to shake hands anymore. They think it spreads germs or diseases to the other person. Problem solved with Peacetime!

Ever since we were kids, we had been doing this Peacetime, mostly with our Mom. I'm pretty sure, however, that anybody could do this with anyone: friends, enemies, strangers, neighbors—anyone really! I definitely think Peacetime is manlier than an Eskimo Kiss, which is rubbing one's nose onto someone ELSE'S nose, who rubs their nose back onto your nose! Who wants to do that, right?

Therefore, you could pretty much give Peacetime to anybody...and be cool about it. In my opinion, now more than ever, the world needs more Peacetime.

UNBELIEVABLY, Grandma wants nothing to do with my Peacetime, and she pushes me away, mostly because SHE HATES ME!

Some of you might ask, "Why does Grandma Bertha hate you, Patrick?" Well, first of all, I'd sincerely like to thank each and every one of you for asking why and for all of your concern. It means soooooo much to me!

Okay, so what happened was really so stupid!

FLASHBACK!

Let's go back, WAY BACK, to the biggest shopping day of the year...Cyber Friday!

Side note: I know it's called Black Friday, but I purposely call it Cyber Friday just to annoy Grandma Bertha who hates technology and shopping online.

It was a very stressful shopping day that brings out the worst in many people. I've always said that Grandma should just avoid this day altogether because she needs to avoid stress, due to some health problems.

Grandma has some digestive problems that cause her to have something called leaky gut syndrome that leads to her having something called leaky bladder syndrome and that eventually leads her to have something called irritable ball syndrome. She basically leaks! Leaks everywhere and leaks everything. EVERYTHING!

This last Cyber Friday, Grandma Bertha and I woke up super stupid early, just to wait OUTSIDE in the

COLD for hours BEFORE the store opened. We did this because she wanted to be first in line. I always go with her because she says she "enjoys my company".

Mom says the only reason Grandma takes me with her is because I'm fast, and I can get to her Cyber Friday deals before they are gone. Whether that is true or not is debatable, BUT I really felt needed and wanted by Grandma. So, it's all good!

She treated me like a King on Cyber Friday mornings. While we were in line she gave me a gallon of green soda and all the Christmas cream filled doughnuts I wanted! Made me feel good. Made me feel awake. Made me feel ALIVE...ROOOOAAAARRRR!

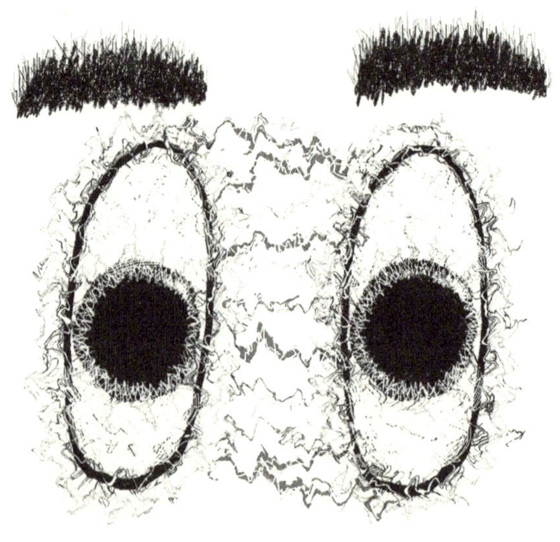

Made me feel like I could bust through the locked doors and grab everything on Grandmas' list, and this guy's list, and that woman's list and that couple's list, and still be in the checkout before Grandma could even reach the first aisle!

WOW, I felt great and it was only 4:45 in the morning! I wanted to start YELLING out a Christmas song. And I started, but then I stopped, only because nobody was joining in.

We had only 15 minutes before the store opens its doors and lets us and the thousands, AND THOUSANDS, of people behind us, flock in and trample one another.

I was so full of excitement that I...I...I didn't know what the heck to do. I turned to Grandma and grabbed both of her shoulders and just shook her, back and forth and back and forth and back and forth and back and forth.

Grandma, we only have 15 minutes left!!

Grandma's smiling face turned into an 'UH OH' kind of face. At the time, I didn't know why her mood suddenly changed. Turns out, I shook a little of the leakiness right out of her!

What are we going to do now? We are trapped!

I began pounding on the main doors. Turns out I was pounding on unbreakable hurricane proof glass doors. Five workers were looking at me from the other side of the doors just shaking their heads. 'Oh, No!' They think I'm trying to bamboozle them and want them to let us come in early, but that's not my intention. Well, actually it was my intention, but only because of Grandma's leaky problem.

I think to myself, 'Maybe they can't hear me through these doors?'

I yelled the words slowly in an effort to warn them that my Grandma had an accident in her pants, and we needed to get into the store right now; otherwise, the smell alone will be devastating to many.

People start moving away from us. On the bright side, at least we have more elbow room. All of a sudden, I felt a whack to the back of my head. "What was that for?" I yelped. "The workers inside can't hear you, but everyone out here can!" Grandma exclaimed.

We only had one other option.

We had to make our way past the thousands, AND THOUSANDS, of people, so we could get to the car and grab a baby wipe or 2 or 20. That way, we could clean up this debacle. Grandma didn't want to go to the car. She wanted to wait and take care of everything when the store opened its doors.

I had a quick talk with her and tried to convince her that its best if we just head to the car. I show her that everyone around us is somehow onto us, but she wants her 60-inch 4K TV.

I reminded her that she is wearing white pants, which would make things a little bit more obvious, but she says she doesn't care and that she wants her coffee machine. I let her know that if we go in that store, she will be leading a trail to the 60-inch 4K TV's and the coffee machines, and it's not going to be a popcorn trail.

People will be stepping in it while slipping and sliding all over it. I asked Grandma if she could handle the breaking news story of the 7 people who are hospitalized from hitting their heads while slipping on her leaky trail of death.

She still wanted to go in, but I just could not let her do that.

I made an executive decision, as I took hold of Grandma's reluctant hand and started parting the sea of people. Then, I shouted warnings of a BIOHAZARD coming through. I tell the population to cover their noses; and please, for the sake of everyone, do not touch us! Amazingly, people didn't heed any of these warnings, so I had to just be as open and as honest as I possibly could be with them.

"MY GRANDMA HAS IRRITABLE BALL SYNDROME, PEOPLE!! LET US THE HECK THROUGH OR I'LL HAVE HER BRUSH UP AGAINST YOU, AS WE PASS ON BY!"

Worked like a charm!

We made it about 30 feet through the crowd when the store decided to open its doors. Here comes the mob...

I quickly turned Grandma around and faced her, so I could create this wedge between us and the herd of oncoming customers. Grandma was slowly lost in the sea of shoppers.

We were no match for this crazy crowd. The stampede trampled Grandma to the ground as the wave of people actually carried me all the way into the store. That was unexpectedly fun!

I debated if I should grab some of the DVD'S that were on sale right next to me, but I had to go back and pick up the remains of my doughnuts. Oh yeah, I also had to help Grandma get up.

She was doing this slow, yet fast, army crawl all the way back up to the doors, as she yells at me for ruining her Cyber Friday. She contorted herself in order to get back into the store.

Her butt really stands out as she crawls. It's quite hypnotizing. Looks like two Mississippi Mountains that are slowly shifting back and forth.

Side note: I really like incorporating the word Mississippi into a sentence. It gives more MEANING to whatever the heck it is that I am saying!

She won't get up.

She just kept crawling and moaning like some scary looking monster. I can't allow her in the store while she's in this condition.

Normally, I would have no chance at dragging Grandma's big butt all the way back to the car, but luckily it's been snowing, and the snow has created a nice slick surface for me to drag Grandma by her feet all the way back to the car! As an added bonus, sliding her on the snow and ice may actually help clean her pants a little bit!

Plus, I knew I looked really strong.

AND that my caring friends, is the story of why Grandma is disgusted with me!

LOL...right?

THE DRIVE

That was then and this is now. Grandma Bertha and I still have the potential to be best of friends, but she can't get over that Cyber Friday ordeal; plus, she simply refuses to go along with what I do and say!

After she gets in the car, we get stuck in the snow, as Dad tries to turn the corner. Can you believe that we're not even 50 feet from her apartment and something terrible has already happened?

This woman is cursed!

I explain to Dad, "It is the extra weight of Grandma in the car that is weighing us down. We have to let her go! It's the only way."

Dad rocks the car back and forth by going in reverse and then not in reverse, reverse and then not reverse, reverse and then not reverse. He informs me that Grandma is staying, and she is not the problem.

He says, "The problem is that nobody has plowed this DARN Street because all the people who PLOW THE STREETS PROBABLY WENT ON STRIKE!"

We finally shake loose and continue on our way.

We should have been to the store by now, BUT Grandma is STARVING and her stomach hurts, so Dad had to make a pit stop and take her to her favorite burger place called, BIG BUNS. How fitting is that? Grandma Bertha is no stranger to BIG BUNS!

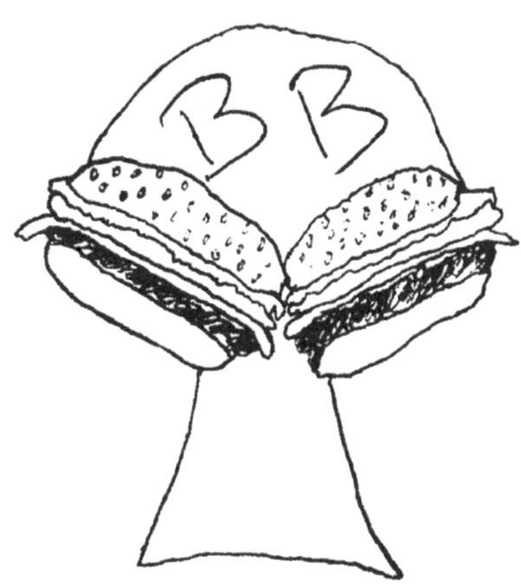

The drive-through line was horribly long and sloppy to drive in with all the snow, but Dad elected to stay in this drive-through line, rather than go inside and order. Which way is the fastest?

This is a big gamble that certainly will drive him crazy!

You see, there is always a possibility that by the time he would get back into the car after going inside the burger place...his spot in the drive-through line would have already been served and long gone. How can one even carry on after something like that happens?

And this has happened a few times in the past. Talk about being paranoid!

FLASHBACK!

Imagine waiting to place your order while you're in line inside, and you see this guy. Let's just call him "Dad".

He is pacing horribly back and forth within a one-foot radius while keeping an eye on where his spot would have been in the drive-through line.

He sees that spot (right behind the big white van) inch up closer and closer and closer.

People don't know that he is watching HIS spot in the drive-through line window.

They are thinking he is getting ready to rob this place!

His blood pressure is ridiculously high right now,

as he gulps and squirms every time that white van moves.

Sweat is building up on his forehead, skin from his lip is being chewed on, fingernails are gnawed until they can't be gnawed anymore, all while talking to himself. If he doesn't look suspicious as all heck, I don't know who does?

Aaaand there goes the white van, pulling away after receiving their order.

That's always the tipping point that leads to him screaming out, "This place sucks! You need to do something about these lines! Horrendous, I tell you! I could have been here and back home by now, if I would have stayed in that drive-through line!"

Anyway, that was then and this is now.

Back in the drive-through line, we pull up to the speaker, so we can order.

Dad NOW asks Grandma what she would like?

NOW?

He asks her, now!

Grandma Bertha stuck her nose against the window in an effort to read the menu.

We just waited in this long line and Dad could have found out what she wanted to order in any of the last 10 minutes or so, but he chose to wait until we got up to the speaker.

After all this time lollygagging around in line, all she wants is ONE cheeseburger, WITHOUT the cheese!

Gunther about had a heart attack because he gladly would have taken the cheese off and eaten it, right then and there for her.

I decided to interrupt and roll down the back window as I start an impromptu order for myself: "Ahhhh yeah, I'll take an extra big, large, GIANT, Grande, Christmas, peppermint, chocolate, mocha, iced coffee with extra whipped cream and 15 cherries on top! Also, can I get that in one of those special Russian mule cups?"

I am smiling from ear to ear, as I look up into the falling snow because I know...THIS is what Christmas actually tastes like!

Dad shouts out the window and tells the woman

that we don't want that special Christmas iced coffee and tells her to take it off the order. He says we don't have the money for it!

$9!

"You mean to tell me that we don't have $9 to pay for one little SPECIAL Christmas iced coffee?" I complain.

Mad Dad says, "No!"

As I'm leaning out the window looking over the menu, Grandma Bertha starts rolling up the window on me. She says that will shut me up. You know what; it did shut me up because I was in shock of the possible suffocation or even my body being decapitated in half!

As I'm fluttering around trying to escape, Dad ordered a coffee—pretty much because he is addicted to coffee.

I try to tell the woman to take HIS coffee off the order because we don't have the money, but Dad already starts pulling away.

He drinks coffee like most other people

drink water.

Large coffee with 6 creams and 6 sugars is his thing.

Do not tell anybody this, but Dad only uses 3 of the creams and 3 of the sugars, and he saves the other 3 creams and 3 sugars for when he needs them at home.

I'm saving that secret of his for when I need to get black mail from him!

Pulling up to the window, the drive-through woman takes his money and gives him his change. She gives him his order...AND UH OHHHH!

He pulls away and then realizes he did not get the

correct amount of change back!

What's this?

He is missing 3 pennies!

If our Mom was in the car with him, she would make his BE–HIND immediately go right back in line and get those 3 pennies! Even if it were one cent, she would make him turn right back around and get the correct amount that he had coming to him!

Side note: Our Mom is the world's biggest nitpicker. She tends to overthink and dissect every little thing until she feels she's made her point perfectly clear. She nitpicks this, she nitpicks that, she nitpicks THIS, and she nitpicks THAT. She nitpicks everything to the point that when she is done nitpicking you, you have no more nits left for her to pick!

But, she was not here, so this time he was lucky!

Luther is begging Dad to let him go in and get those 3 pennies back. With the most sinister look, Luther begs Dad, "Please let me go in there and handle this. I'll not only get your 3 pennies back, I'll get interest on it, plus Patrick's Christmas

Coffee drink!"

Suddenly, I take Luther's' side on this one, BUT Dad doesn't care about the 3 "LITTLE" pennies, so he just tells us to simmer down.

We pull over so Dad can hand Grandma her cheeseburger, minus the cheese; and also, so he can fix his coffee.

We have no useable cup holders because they are filled to the rim with junk and stuff, so Dad decides to put his cup of coffee up onto the dashboard.

I don't have a rocket scientist kit or anything like that, but I'm not sure I would have put a cup of scalding hot coffee on a SLANTED dashboard?

That's just me though. I wouldn't do it.

I take Grandma's cheeseburger from Dad and hold it out for her to take, but she does not take it.

Grandma doesn't look so well.

Her eyes are closed and her head is flopped to one side. I THINK she is sleeping, but I'm not sure? How could she fall asleep so quickly?

She is pressed up against me. I am nice and warm, so she could be feeling all snuggly and cozy right now; but still, is something wrong with her?

I look at her from head to toe and nothing at all is moving.

Her arms are crossed and covering her stomach, so I can't really tell if her stomach is moving to indicate that she is breathing or not.

I am a little worried, but not that much because I know that this is all in my head.

I'm cool as a cucumber, as I gaze over at her. I am watching her through the corner of my eyes and nudging her with my elbow, but there is no movement.

I take my 2 fingers and put them on her knuckles, so I can check for a pulse.

Nothing.

I check again at various locations of her biceps and a 3rd time under her underarm, but no luck at all.

I'm not even sure what it is that I'm feeling for,

but I think those places seem to be somewhat familiar places of importance. Should I try her bingo wings?

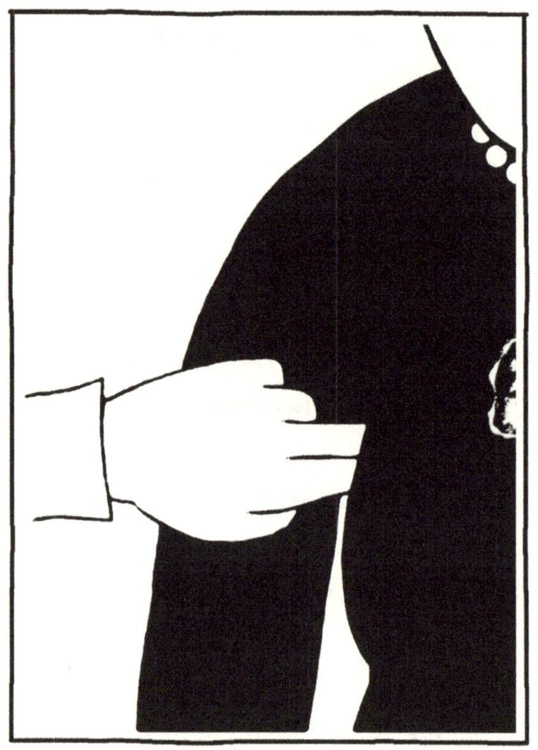

Usually, I move from seat to seat on these car rides because I just can't sit still. Right now, I want to move, but I'm paralyzed in some exciting fear.

With every nudge I make and every glance I take, I'm watching her through my peripheral vision, yet nothing.

The final straw was when I gave her a sudden HARD nudge to the ribs, and then I saw her head fall back in my direction with her eyes still closed as her mouth shot open. That's when I knew she was gone.

That's it!

"MOTHER DUCKY! GET ME THE HECK OUT OF THIS CAR!"

There is no place for me to go...especially over her dead body!

I'm trying to get to that front seat, but with all the people and garbage in my way, I don't know who or what I'm stepping on. I feel like I'm running on an oil slick and getting nowhere.

I must have bumped our Dad into the steering wheel and that's when his scalding hot coffee slid off the dashboard and onto his lap.

My screams were sickening.

My Dad's screams from his burned lap were LOUD and just as sickening as my own screams.

The screeches from my Grandma, who rose from

the dead, were pure wicked, especially since she was looking right at me.

I tried to apologize to Mad Dad for accidentally kicking the steering wheel and knocking his coffee onto his lap; and at the same time, I apologized to Grandma for slapping her just to make sure she wasn't in a zombie state.

Sorry...Slap!

Sorry...Slap!

Sorry...Slap!

I knew that she hated me and that it was I who would be the first one that she would seek out and try to eat, so I had to find out if she was or was not a zombie.

I told her to say something—anything—because I'm pretty much a zombie expert and I knew that zombies couldn't talk; only humans can talk.

And I kept slapping her until she answered my questions.

1) How many sleepwalkers have you killed?

2) How many people persons have you killed?

3) If Peter Piper PECKED a pack of pickles, how many PIMPLES did Peter POPPER PICK?

And why?

Her answer was, "STOP hitting me, you MANIAC!"

That was not even close to the right answer, but I'll accept it under these circumstances.

Dad was in so much pain and was so upset that for a few moments he was Ruffin and Scruffin everything and anything.

Side note: Ruffin and Scruffin is a PG-13 version of how I describe my mad dad's trucker mouth.

I tried to distract him and tell him it was a Christmas miracle that Grandma was even alive!

Eyes closed and not doing well, he repeated that she was taking a Ruffin Scruffin nap!

Our focus turned to Dad, who was feeling the

effects of some spilled piping hot coffee!

He was squirming in his seat while repeatedly yelling out "It's hot! It's hot!"

We have never EVER heard our Dad scream like how he screamed right there!

He just tortured himself for no reason at all with that coffee!

Also, this is kind of ironic because I remember burning MY tongue once while trying a sip of my DAD'S coffee and I said the same thing, "It's hot! It's hot!"

Luckily, it was snowing out; and fortunately, I was gifted with some quick reflexes, both mentally and physically.

As I'm thinking about what I should do to help treat a person who spilled hot coffee in one's lap, I hop out of the passenger side of the car, try to jump onto the hood, but slid all the way down.

These conditions are not made for one trying to slide across a car hood in hopes of helping to save someone!

I tried to crawl back up the hood, but the snow-covered car was just too slick and would not allow it. I felt like one of those kids who try to walk up a slide with socks on, but just can't seem to make it to the top.

I was almost to Dad's door when my OCD kicked in.

I had to go back to my door that I just came out of to make sure it was closed all the way.

I headed back towards our Dad, but again I had to

go back and double check that my door was indeed closed all the way.

I couldn't quite make it to Dad's door, as I had to keep going back to triple and quadruple check to see if my door was indeed closed or if it came open for some reason.

I don't even really care if the door is opened or closed, but I uncontrollably feel the need to keep checking on this dang door.

I truly know this would have gone on and on if it weren't for Dad shouting out, "What the HECK are you doing?"

His voice kind of woke me up and out of that OCD trance I was in.

Finally, I ran around the car and opened his door up while at the same time I scooped up all this snow and threw it on him and his burned area.

He stopped screaming. I don't know if it was because I was helping lower the temperature of his leg area, or if it was because he was in such disbelief of how much snow I was able to dump onto him in such a short amount of time.

I just kept throwing and throwing armfuls of snow all up in there, until he screamed for me to stop.

I was like a dog in the backyard trying to dig a hole to bury his bone, or a cat in a litter box trying to cover his poop!

I fired one last snowball for good luck, then, I hopped back into the car.

Dad says it's nothing bad, but I assume he has 3rd or 4th or 5th grade degree burns on his thighs... something like that?

We try to talk him out of going shopping because he is in no condition to do so; but like a tough son of a gun, he refuses to go home empty handed.

Slipping and sliding on the snow-covered streets, we head west to go shopping for our Christmas dinner and any last-minute surprise gifts!

THE YELLOW STORE

Finally, we arrived at our store, or at least we arrived at the parking lot of our store, the YELLOW Store! We call it the Yellow Store because everything in there is yellow! The walls, shelves and even many item labels are all yellow. Looks like the color of your pee when you're dehydrated.

Everything in here is cheap off brands or generic items, which is perfect for a large family like ours.

Did I mention that our Dad HATES going shopping, and he especially HATES going shopping on Saturdays because everybody goes shopping on Saturdays? Well today, it's so crowded, you can't even move!

He thought we were going to get lucky because he thought the snow would keep people away, but guess again.

It's worse than even he could've imagined.

He thinks EVERYBODY from the surrounding suburbs is at the Yellow Store at the same time, which is right now.

Ha Ha, it only looks that way because the Yellow Store that we used to frequent closed down and moved into its newest location, right here, in the middle of the largest mall in Illinois!

We slowly drive the outskirts of the mall, searching all the rows, going up and down and all around for at least 30 minutes.

We have not even come close to finding anything, but on the bright side we do get to drive past the Yellow Store's BIG Christmas tree a few times.

What a sight to see! Every hour on the hour they put on this glorious display, as they synchronize Christmas music with moving lights that dance to the music.

Luther constantly holds out his hand in the tree's direction. He says he is trying to use his Christmas wish to move the big tree.

Side note: Luther has been wishing for the ability to be able to move objects with his mind power!

He grunts and strains with all his might in his attempts to move the tree.

As we drive, we debate if the tree is real or fake? All of us, except for Luther, think it's a fake tree. He insists the tree is real and because it's real it's heavier, and because it's heavier, that is the reason why he cannot move the tree with his mind power!

Luther shouts out to the heavens, "THIS TREE WILL MOOOOVE BECAUSE OF MY MINNNNNDDD POWERRRRR!"

His very confident moment ends rather abruptly when Dad's frustration of not getting a parking spot takes over.

Dad sees somebody pulling out leaving a parking spot wide open. The problem is somebody else also sees this same parking spot. And, the race is on!

Herking and jerking, stopping and starting, breaking and going...he's a mad man! What the heck just happened in the last 10 seconds?

Dad is very lucky the other person stopped and let him take the spot because he was 100% not stopping before he was fully in that spot!

I think I have whiplash from all the sudden jerky breaking!

Grandma does not want to go into the store with us because her stomach is upset. I thought I smelled something after she came back to life, so she wants to stay in the car.

Luther, who lost a quick yet intense game of paper-rock-scissors-baseball, is the one who has to stay in the car to keep Grandma some company!

Side note: Paper-rock-scissors-baseball is a game I invented. The baseball is like a wild card, and I can use it to top any of the other symbols at any other time. The symbol looks like you're holding a baseball. The key to this version is to only play it with the ones you feel like you have an advantage over. I seek out the younger, SLOWER ones. They never know what the heck is going on!

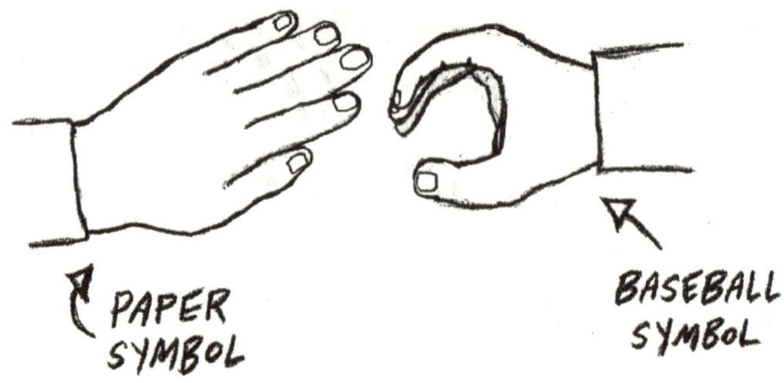

I also do really well at regular Paper-rock-scissors.

FYI, my secret for always winning regular paper-rock-scissors is that I just quickly jumble up my hand so it forms a little bit of rock, with a little bit of paper, mixed with a little dash of scissors.

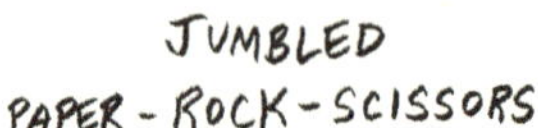

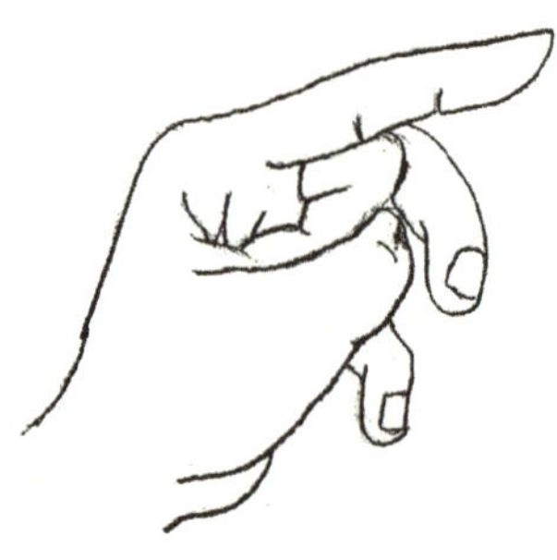

You can't really tell what the heck symbol I just made!

Grandma asks me if I was making gang signs again?

I give her a mad stare for 5 seconds.

She looks away because nobody can handle my mad stares!

Side note: Mad stares have been, and always will be, a strength of mine!

As we're leaving the car, Grandma Bertha happily yells out, "OK, don't forget that allll I want for Christmas is something that is shiny and that goes really, really fast—like 0 to 300 in 5.8 seconds, fast!"

She does her little laugh, but I don't get it.

Just before Gertrude closes the door, I ask Grandma Bertha, "why would you want a scale for Christmas?"

Then, I leave. I wouldn't want a scale as a Christmas present; but I guess, that's what makes the world go round.

As I look back at the car, poor Luther looks like we just left him behind in jail! Plus, Grandma looks super-duper mad for some reason?

I feel his pain because I know I would not want to be left behind locked in the car with Grandma Bertha either!

Now he's screaming and banging on the fogged-up window, trying to convince us he has to pee really bad. We might have believed him if he wasn't known as the little boy who cries at wolves (a.k.a. Mr. April Fools) all the time!

Good luck Luther, we will be back sometime later today!

As we head into the store, I can clearly overhear our Dad asking Gertrude what she wants for Christmas, and I can clearly hear her tell him that she doesn't need anything, as long as she has her family.

I'll say a prayer for Gertrude because clearly something is wrong with her.

Dad gives her a big hug as he says to her, "And that's why you have always been MY favorite. Plus, we always save a bunch of money on you!"

They both share a laugh together; although, Gertrude seems puzzled, wondering if there is any truth to that, or not.

I decide to stop for one second, so I can put a quarter into the red kettle pot right here outside the store. I take a quick selfie of me, as I put that quarter into the slot.

Instead of saying, "Cheese", I say, "This one is for you, little Timmy!"

This makes for a great picture of me to post online when I get back home. Giving money to these kettles, or to the homeless, or to random elderly people isn't quite the same unless I openly get credit for it.

Right?

I always want to give because it makes me feel good, but if our Dad or our Mom ground me from my phone and therefore I can't take a picture of the "Giving Patrick Situation", well only our Mom and our Dad are to blame. Those...selfish...jerks. That came out bad, so I look up to the heavens and apologize to Santa!

Shopping with us is a little bit different than going shopping with your typical family.

We have such a big household that we have multiple carts that we fill to the max! On average we fill up between 3 and 5 full shopping carts. Today, I have 2 carts and Dad has 2 carts.

I feel bad for him because he still looks like he is in agony. He also seems flustered trying to juggle multiple shopping lists and hang onto the pen he uses to mark off items.

Gunther, who somehow squeezed into the shopping cart seat, keeps grabbing at our Dad's shopping list, getting him even more frustrated.

Another thing about Dad going shopping and why it's rather stressful for him is that he CANNOT miss anything on that list, otherwise he has some "splaining" to do to our Mom when he gets home!

It's hot and we are starting to sweat, so I suggest that we all just take our coats off and cool down a little.

Not to jinx this thing, but so far...everything is...so good.

Gunther is now sitting in one of my carts, after Dad couldn't take him anymore. I don't know what it is, but he is leaning over and eating something right from Dad's cart.

Also, Gertrude looks content riding one of those stick-horses between Dad's shopping carts.

Dad is struggling mightily with his grocery lists and Gunther squirming all over the place in one of the shopping carts.

I'm mature, and my carts were already full of groceries, so I decide to take some of the pressure off Dad. I yell out to him that I could take Gertrude and Gunther, so he can concentrate on doing his shopping.

I only yell to increase the odds of God, Santa, and Dad all hearing my kind act.

He said, "Yeah, yeah, yeah that sounds good," as he shooed me away.

Ideas come aplenty in my head, and I have a doozy right now!

I grab me a few of those kid cages and combine them to form an octagon playpen and bring them over towards a main aisle. It's a heavy traffic area, but the only place to accommodate the octagon cage and still allow for people to get their shopping carts past.

I enclose Gertrude, Gunther and me in our quick set-up daycare area.

I throw in some toys and some snacks from the adjacent aisles and...WHAAAAA LAAAAAA; we're all set!

An 8 pack of paper towels serves as a great seat for me, as I do some people watching.

I let parents passing by know that I can include their kids for $5 BUT, only if their kid is not an idiot.

Snacks ARE included!

Normally, I don't watch any of these little toddling kids because my thing is, I don't watch anybody who can't talk!

Money talks though; so, bring them on!

One woman dropped off her 3 kids and gave me $15 dollars!

I was so happy that I just made some money, and she was so happy that I could help her out of this bind.

We were both so happy that I grabbed her by her face, and I went in for...some Peacetime.

I could tell that she was not in a Peacetime mood because she spun away and backed off me.

She did tell me that she would be back soon, and she did give me one of those awkward semi quick parting hugs. "Well worth the money" was her happy quote.

That gave me an idea.

I see a white board near aisle 5 and write down her quote and use it as my first testimony.

WOW, I'm surprised at all the people who are willing to just hand over their kids to me. I am wearing a yellow shirt, so I wonder if these people think that I actually work here or something?

Side note: Whatever store we go to, I always try to wear the same color shirt the employees wear. Just...you know, to kind of fit in. I feel needed when people ask me any and all kinds of questions.

I ALWAYS give these people an answer, whether I know the answer or not. And I'll be honest with you; aisle 7 is my go-to aisle of choice. I don't know where ANYTHING is, so no matter what a person asks me for; I almost always tell them that they can find it in aisle 7!

I randomly tell other workers, "Hey, it's better to give the people an answer than to not give the people an answer, and if you don't know the answer then just make up the answer!"

Customers who come up to me thinking I work there never know what reaction they will be receiving. As long as I'm in a good mood, hey...it's cool. BUT DO NOT APPROACH ME when I'm in a bad mood! I'll say to you what all the disgruntled employees really want to say to you.

Back to Patrick's daycare.

Within minutes I have to start turning people away.

Also, one youngster WAS an idiot, so I had to remove him from the octagon. "Hit the road kid; YOU'RE OUTTA HERE!" I told him.

Business was doing really well for those 10 to 15 minutes, BUT I had to close down shop because I noticed that the Yellow Store had an unexpected surprise guest in the area.

SANTA!

As I open up the cage door, I tell all the kids to go find their parents or guardians and I wish that 2-year-old good luck, as Gertrude, Gunther and I make a beeline towards Santa.

Wow, Santa is in the store AND there is nobody in line?

What an unexpected bonus!

Probably nobody is in line because the Yellow Store's Santa is wearing an all yellow Santa's outfit. Why would they do that to Santa? Looks a little odd.

Santa looks annoyed right now because we interrupted his conversation with the smiling elf woman.

As I approach, I tell Santa that this is Gertrude, as I help guide her up to his chair.

Seems like Gertrude accidentally poked Santa with her stick-horse, as she was backing up to sit on his lap.

He gave a weak "ho, ho, ho," as he holds his gut and asks her what she wants for Christmas.

I know that this is the "helping" Santa and not the REAL SANTA, so I'm just playing along, winking at him occasionally to give him the sign that I know who he is and what is going on!

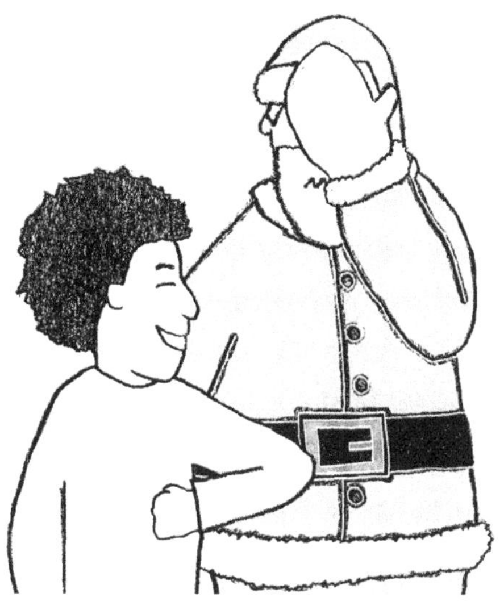

I tell him that I was once a Santa's helper just like him, as I whip out a picture of me all dressed up just like him.

In that picture, I'm smiling, giving a thumbs up, and you can definitely tell that it is me because you can see my flannel shirt hanging out all over the place! I was just Santa's helper, but it felt good!

Santa asks, "So, Gertrude, what do you want for Christmas?"

She tells him that even though she just told our Dad that she doesn't need anything, she does LOVE this horse.

As she hugs the life out of the stick-horse, she falls sloooowly off his lap and to the ground.

Climbing back up onto Santa's lap, she tells him, "What I really want is a little Kylee or Avery doll from the Kylee and Avery Doll Collection, BUT my Mom won't let me get one."

A confused Santa looks over at me; I give him another wink to let him know that I know about him. And then he asks Gertrude, "Why won't your Mother let you get one?"

She said, "I don't know. I think it might be because I already have over 100 of them!"

He looks over at me as he tells her, "Well, I'll see what I can do."

I smile and wink once more, but I don't know if he knows why I'm winking at him?

He keeps giving me weird looks!

He lets Gertrude off his lap and tells her the whole "Be good and leave out cookies" for him and all the blah-blah-blah usual stuff Santa says.

NOW, its Gunther's turn, but before I take him out of the cart, I have to take the bag of grapes away from him because he is eating all of them.

They are not even washed!

Our Mom would have a heart attack if she knew he was eating fruit without it being washed off first.

While putting Gunther onto Santa's lap, I wink and introduce him by whispering, "This is Gunther" into Santa's ear.

Gunther has not looked up yet.

He is too preoccupied with eating grapes to realize where he is and who this is. All he knows is that he is sitting on someone's lap.

"Ho! Ho! Ho!"

After the first "Ho," Gunther freezes and stops eating the grapes.

After the second "Ho," Gunther levels his head and his eyes are wide open.

After the third "Ho," Gunther looks up and recognizes that it is Santa! I will never forget this moment!

Yes, I did know that Gunther had bad experiences

with Santa in the past, but I thought for sure he would have outgrown his fear, since the last time he saw Santa was at least 2 weeks ago.

You never know what is going to happen in these situations, and that's why I took out my phone to record it.

I wonder which came first: the scream or the pee?

Well, since I'm recording, we can find out the answer and more when we watch it later, as soon as we get back home!

As I take Gunther away from Santa, I decide not to wink at him this time. It is a great decision in my opinion, since Santa is sitting there with his arms up in disbelief, all SOAKED in Gunther pee.

Dad shows up, just in the St. Nick of time, to help me with Gunther.

I tell Dad there is good news and there is bad news.

The good news is that Gertrude was excellent for Santa. NEVER a problem! She asked him for a Kylee or Avery doll and Santa told her that he would see what he could do.

Dad sighs and then asks, "And the bad news?"

The bad news is that Gunther ate half the grapes.

And he peed all over Santa!

Technically, I don't know if ALL that pee is ONLY from Gunther because, if you look at it, it sure does look like a big mess!

Mmmm hmmmm! All dressed up in yellow, trying to camouflage everything. A little too convenient if you ask me.

This Santa appears to be in a sour mood because of my statement. I'm not even going to bother telling him what I want for Christmas right now because I think he will do something to it.

Dad's favorite word is MOTHER, and he says that word quite a few times as he tries to figure out how and where to pick up Gunther.

Santa is saying Mother as well, but for different reasons.

It is like they have some contest of who could say Mother the most and the scariest?

On the positive side, Gunther got some new clothes and Dad was all done with his shopping!

Dad told Gertrude that she could ride on the stick-horse until we get to the checkout, and then she would have to give it to the worker to put back on the shelf.

To take Gertrude's mind off of it, I ask her to show me how fast she can make it around the store and back with that stick-horse.

ANNNNND she's off!

Now Dad won't have to deal with any begging and pleading!

Can you believe with all these people waiting, they ONLY have 10 lines open?

Do you know how I know that?

Well, our Dad has been mumbling this for the last few minutes, while we're stuck waiting in this long checkout line.

He doesn't have any patience at all for this.

He is even telling the woman who is holding 2 gallons of milk moaning and sighing behind us that he can't believe they only have 10 lines open!

He says, "This is poor management! They can clearly see the lines are backed up and go all the way down the food aisles. They clearly need to open more registers. Poor management!"

I lean in and whisper, "Dad, why don't you just let this poor woman get in front of us?" I throw in the word "poor" in hopes of making Dad feel bad for her.

Dad exclaims, "Normally, I don't do this and usually I would let her in, BUT she has another thing coming if she thinks she is getting in front of us!"

In my head I am thinking, "Normally, I don't do this and usually I would let her in? Really?"

I have never in all my life seen my Dad let anybody cut in front of him!

Anywhere!

Ever!

So, just an FYI to that woman with the 2 gallons of milk standing behind us, you shall not pass!

My Dad is talking to her, telling her all of this information, but what he is really doing is sizing her up, watching her closely so she won't get any fancy schmancy ideas to cut in front of us!

Don't you think it's a little odd that wherever you move, he is right in front of you... wherever you are?

Don't you think it's odd that while he is talking to you, his arms are spread open a little unusually wide right now?

I know what my Dad is thinking. His view is that you and your 2 gallons of milk are equal to our 4 full shopping carts of food. If you wanted to get in front of us, you should have been here before us.

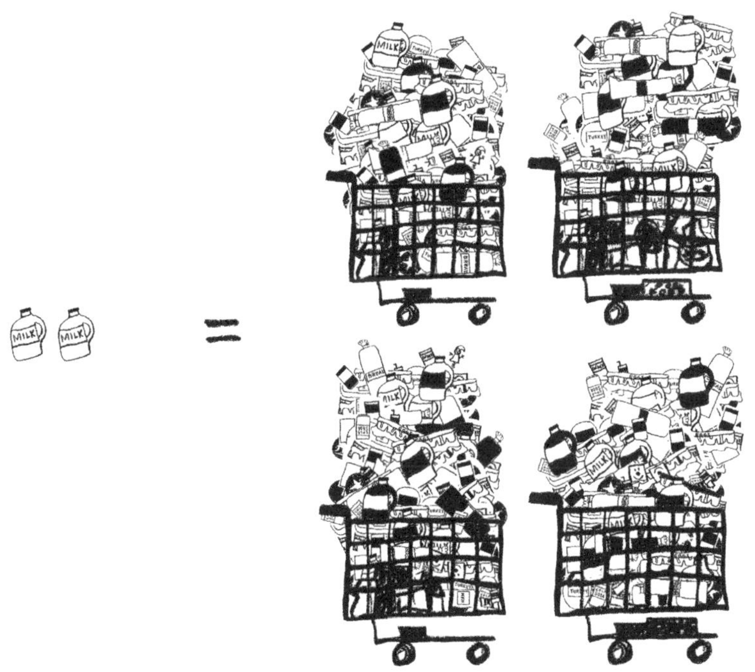

I can tell she is agitated and annoyed due to her sniffling and snorting and whining sounds, so I want to make her feel better.

I turn and whisper to her, "It's nothing against you...personally."

I turn and whisper to her, "He's very territorial."

I turn and whisper to her, "He's like a dog defending his area." I even lift my leg to show her about marking someone's territory.

She is not engaged in my conversation, so I ask her a question: "Guess what?"

She rolls her eyes and replies, "What?"

I say, "Grandma Bertha has a big butt!"

I think that is FUNNY, but this woman does not see it the same way that I do!

Our Mom says, "Women appreciate honesty." So, I turn and whisper to her, "I give you a 5, on a scale of 1–10. Maybe a 4 if I wore glasses, but I don't even wear glasses."

I don't think she is appreciating my honesty, right now! This woman is visibly upset and wants to get in front of us or away from us, in the worst way!

Unspoken proper grocery store checkout line etiquette from the "Unspoken Proper Grocery Store Checkout Line Etiquette" magazine says–if you have a gazillion groceries in your cart(s) and the person behind you only has 1 or 2 or just a few groceries, you should allow them to bypass you and take your position in line.

That's what the "Unspoken Proper Grocery Store Checkout Line Etiquette" magazine says.

Then, the woman does something that I have never seen anyone ever do before. She actually asks our Dad if she can cut in front of him!

Most people would let her go and even I would let her move in front of us.

I would, but not our Dad!

There isn't any way in heck that you or anyone can go ahead of us. Not while our Dad is right here watching you from the corners of his eyes!

"NO CUTSIES, WOMAN!" Was Dad's heartfelt to the point reply.

No cutsies...until the cashier yells for us to let her go by because "she only has 2 items."

As "No Cutsies" woman moves in front of us, Dad's scowling eyeballs go back and forth between the cashier and "No Cutsies" woman.

Dad doesn't know what the heck to do now, so he just licks his lips. This woman was just granted permission to pass us up.

As words are building up and about to come out of Dad's mouth, there is an awkward silence.

Then, a few slow "MOTHERS" sputter out, followed by "Maybe you should have more than just 10 lanes open!" our Dad yells back to the cashier! He tells me and everyone who would listen to him that there is no excuse for this to be happening right now.

I try to hide from all the attention our Dad is drawing to us because we look like BILLYS...from the hill, but there is no place to escape.

We're surrounded by four full overflowing carts, a Mad Dad, a kid running circles around the shopping cart on her horse, and another kid who smells like pee and is eating the deli ham right out of the bag!

I tell Gertrude to go do another lap!

Then, I tell Dad that Gunther is eating the dang ham right out of the bag!

"Well get the dang ham away from him" he says angrily.

He yells at me, so naturally I have to yell at Gunther!

"Gunther, give me the DANG HAM!" He is eating it like it's a sandwich, only there is no bread! It's just layers of HAM!

The "No Cutsies" woman keeps shaking her head like she's ashamed to be next to us.

I know she is telling the cashier that I put that half-eaten bag of ham on the bubblegum display next to our cart because I keep seeing them look in our direction.

I boldly say, "We don't want that ham now!"

I did put that ham on the rack, but Miss "No Cutsies" should not have ratted us out, especially after we were kind enough to indirectly let her go in front of us!

I say out loud, "Listen lady, just because it's

Christmas Eve, do not think for one second that Santa or his dwarves are that busy that they cannot see or hear you talking about us behind his back."

She responds with a head shake and double eye roll.

Now she's just an idiot, so when they ask her for her phone number, she whispers to them "598-03...." She's lucky she mumbled the last two digits.

Trying to whisper...when I have ears like an EAGLE! I do an eagle screech just to let her know that was stupid!

I just keep on repeating it out loud.

"598-03 something something.

"598-03 something something.

"598-03 something something."

SHE DOES NOT LIKE IT!

As she leaves, I say goodbye and that I'll call her sometime!

I don't know what this world has come to, but the Yellow Store we visit makes YOU bag your OWN groceries!

What the heck, Yellow Store!

That's what you have employees for. Don't get lazy on us!

I don't like it...I don't know how to do it...AND it flusters the heck out of me.

I feel like people are watching me and mocking my inexperienced bagging skills.

I AM AN ATHLETE, a great, great athlete, but for some reason bagging groceries does not come easy to me.

Our Dad and I come from different schools of bagging.

Dad went to the 'everything has to go in a specific order' school! Mr. Perfection stacks breads and chips in one bag and canned goods or anything heavy goes in the other 'doubled' bags.

Now, I, on the other hand, went to the 'throwing as many darn items in the bag as humanly possible' school!

Also, I don't do 'doubled' bags!

Our Dad is making me look like a fool.

He has this cool bartender flip, where he gracefully tosses up can after can to his other hand that is stationed in the paper bag. Finally, he catches those cans and smoothly places them into the bag—like a boss.

I try this and the cans drop and clank everywhere.

I'm not even touching some of these cans, as I struggle to throw them to myself.

How I hit that window with a can of sweet peas is beyond me!

I focus and pretend like I am giving myself an alley-oop, as I gently tip a can into the bag. Occasionally, I set myself up nicely and do a vicious slam dunk, but that doesn't happen too often.

I guess this must be something that becomes easier as you get older—like an elderly skill that I will inherit when I am old like my Dad. I must be talking out loud because Dad says that he is not old.

How can this man even hear me when he is focused on bagging food? He is multitasking to the max. I don't understand...he has 4 bags done and I only have half of a bag done.

That's it!

My new bagging philosophy goal is that whatever is next, within my reach, goes in the bag.

Always set goals, people, just so you can obtain them!

If I have to look like I am a Mississippi mudslinger who is slinging mud all over the continental Mississippi River...then so be it!

I am not playing around here anymore as I use the scoop, lift and drop technique.

However, I feel like I'm in a bagging contest with our Dad! And I am sure I'm in some kind of contest; yes, I know I am because I see Dad watching me as I am watching him! His tongue is even hanging out of the corner of his mouth and he has his game face on.

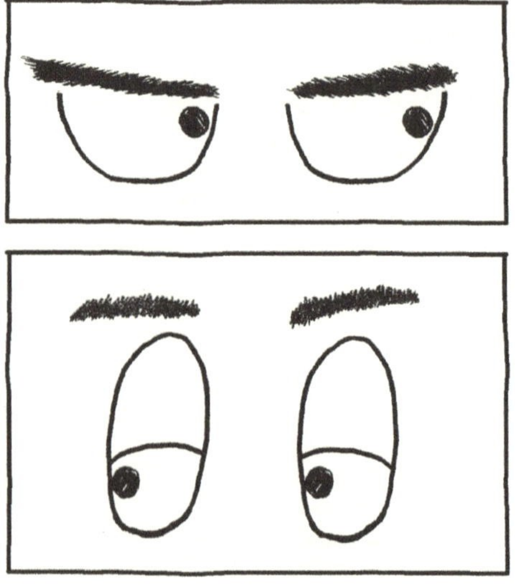

You would think Father would be happy to see me complete my grocery bag fulfillments, as I ask him what is taking him so long.

He looks very, very worried right now, as we leave the building.

THE PARKING LOT

It takes some serious skill to be able to push and pull 2 full shopping carts from the store through the snowy parking lot, around Chewing Gum Mountain, over Chocolate-covered Raisin River and finally to our sucky station wagon! This is partly why I was chosen as the first overall pick in the draft.

Surprise, surprise! We can't find our car, AGAIN! Dad gets so upset when this happens, and it happens a lot!

Dad's first excuse is: "The snow is coming down so strong right now that it's hindering our vision. It is big with chunky chunks and nobody can see through this." Lame excuse, if you ask me.

Dad's second excuse is to blame me. He says "Why don't YOU know where we parked? I thought you were keeping track of that!"

CAN YOU BELIEVE THAT? Blaming me for his poor locating senses! I don't know where the heck he parked! He knows I don't pay attention. Plus, this parking lot is GIGANTIC!

I say, "How do you expect me to remember which parking spot WE parked in? Huh? There must be close to 10,000 parking spots here, Dad!"

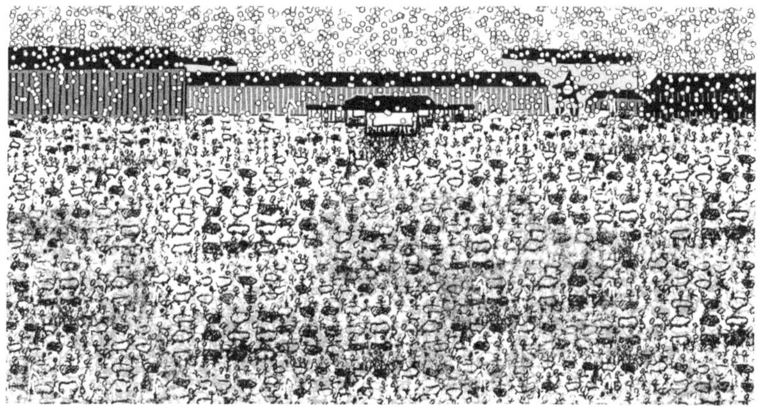

Looking around he says, "I remember when I got out of the car, I saw the Yellow Store's big Christmas tree off in the distance. BUT either it disappeared or it's snowing so hard that I can't even see it? Let's just keep looking."

"HA! You know what Dad; I'll just find the car," I reply.

MAN, you know what? My dad is right. Actually, the snow IS coming down so strong right now that it IS hindering our vision. It IS big with chunky chunks and nobody can see through this. I tell him, "Forget it. You find it."

He insists that we both look for it.

So, I take one side of the aisle and he takes the other.

I wish we had one of those car remotes that make the "BEEP BEEP" sound when you click the remote, but we don't have one.

No luck, and we have been stranded for what feels like hours. So, the next best thing is to shout for 'HELP'. I can't even shout for help because the snow is blowing into my mouth every time I attempt to say it.

All that is coming out is "Helpffth! Helpffth! Helpffth!"

Some guy runs over towards me and asks me if I need help.

Startled, I told him no and for him to get the heck away from me!

STRANGER DANGER!

That's when I hear the third excuse. A predictable dad says, "Someone moved the car! AGAIN!" This is by far his most popular excuse.

Our Dad is convinced that someone moved his car because he is so POSITIVE that he parked it right here, somewhere in this area.

I ask him if he really thinks that someone follows him to wherever he is going, then that person waits until he gets into the store, hotwires his car, and then moves it to a different parking spot—just to mess with him.

A defeated Dad says, "You never know; nothing would surprise me anymore!"

I am shocked by this response. I thought he would have been mad at me for asking such a smart aleck question, but because he answered so calmly and sincerely, he is making me think there is a possibility that this could be happening.

Who would move our car?

Grandma Bertha?

Petunia?

Maybe the football referee our Dad blames for everything?

Bandits?

Clowns?

Suddenly, and oddly, Luther comes running by us and says he knows where the car is.

Dad yells at Luther as he speeds past us, "Luther what are you doing out of the car? You're supposed to be with your Grandma!"

An excited Luther tells us, "I couldn't move the tree with my mind, so I went to see if I could move the tree with my body. I just wanted to see if I could climb to the top of the Yellow Store's big Christmas tree...and I did. I made it all the way to the top and touched the star. I was even climbing to the synchronized music! I started shaking the top of the tree to the beat of the music when all of a sudden, the tree fell. I didn't even get hurt. It was like an angel just gently laid me down on top of some innocent bystander! It was awesome! C'mon, the car is this way!"

Both Dad and I have no idea what just happened.

Our focus is on following Luther back to the car.

We are close to our car, 4 rows over and about 15 car lengths down.

The race is now on. It's me and my shopping carts

vs. Dad and his shopping carts, and the first one to the car is the winner.

If you have ever seen one of those videos where there is a really bad car pileup because no cars can stop in the snow, well, that's what Dad and I look like as we hit the side of our station wagon with 4 full shopping carts.

We could not stop for anything!

That woke Grandma up from her sixth nap of the day.

There is minimal damage to the car from the shopping carts. We only have stupid dents and scratches all over the side, along with a busted side mirror.

Dad is a little more negative about it as he stomps on an open soda can. That can must have been full, because soda was flying all over him and the car. It could have been worse.

Most importantly is that nobody was hurt, except for Grandma, who was sleeping up against the door that we rammed into with the carts. So, she might have a headache or a concussion, but everything else is good.

I guess we should have thought out how we're going to fit all these groceries into the car with all these people in here.

Where there is a will, there is a way, I say!

I get a head nod of approval from Dad who starts loading up the back of the wagon.

I tell Grandma Bertha to either "open your arms up wide so you can hold all these groceries or scooch on down so I can have room to pile them up next to you."

I kind of force the issue, as I start to pile up a good amount of grocery bags all around her. If she doesn't move, everything will be fine.

Why is Dad sniffing around the back of the station wagon?

Dad accidentally slips and falls in all this yellow snow by the car. There is even a yellow "Luther was here!" spelled out in the snow. Dad is livid at Luther, who denies he did it. A defensive Luther exclaims, "Whoa, whoa, whoa, whoa!! That's definitely not my handwriting!"

Poor Dad, it looks like he just wants to pull his hair out. I wouldn't do that right now, especially since he has Luther pee on his hands.

As the number one draft pick, I earn my non-existing money again by asking, "Dad, we did bring Gertrude with us, right?"

That's what number one draft picks do. We ask the questions!

Dad exclaims, "You know that we brought Gertrude with us!"

"Ok, that's what I thought."

He starts pulling away from his parking spot and heading down the row...and that's when it dawns on him that maybe, just maybe, his oldest son is onto something!

He gave a quick look back at all of us, followed by a loud "OH, SHOOT!"

I know Dad appreciates the information, as I signal to him with a quick fist pump hit to my chest and then the long-distance version of Peacetime, as I spell out peace with my nose in his direction. This is my way of letting him know that I've got his back.

There's no way that our Dad can find a parking spot, so he just parks right smack dab in the middle of whatever aisle we are in. I think it's aisle 7. As he puts the car back into park, I can hear his heart pumping faster and faster.

I see little balls of sweat instantly form all over his head in a calm fear. Turning around again to scan the back seat, his face has a nervous smile and then he quickly leaves the car to go back into the store to find Gertrude.

A few minutes and multiple car honks later, he comes back with her and makes us all laugh by saying that he thought Gertrude was the bag with the pineapple sticking out of it!

"I can see that; I can see that!" Luther says.

I wonder if Dad did or did not pay for that stick-horse Gertrude brought back to the car with her.

Same thing goes for Gunther's new outfit!

As we leave the parking lot, we slowly drive by and gaze at all the police cars that are surrounding the Yellow Store's big Christmas tree that is lying on its side. Luther is sooo happy, so he is trying to record all the commotion. "You see that tree, see that tree? I did that! That is from me!"

As we pass on by, Dad tries to cover up his face, as he doesn't want anyone to know that he is now an accomplice. The rest of us are in awe, however, and think this is the most fantastic display of lights that anyone can ever witness!

Luther says, "And, oh, by the way, the tree is real... and it's marvelous!"

Finally, we are done shopping, and I must say everything went a lot smoother than what I had anticipated.

GO FOR DISPATCH

The way our Dad is driving, you would never know that there is a severe snowstorm going on right now!

Dad says, "I do not understand why people drive so slow when it is snowing out. Irritates the heck out of me!"

He says this as he slips and slides all the way up to the stoplight.

What irritates me is when we are the first at the stoplight and another car pulls up right next to us. Our Dad automatically thinks the person wants to race and get in front of him.

He cannot stand it when somebody passes him, for any reason.

And the light turns green.

This guy who has to get over before his lane ends is waving to thank our Dad as he tries to pass him, but our Dad has other thoughts, as he speeds up to keep even with this guy.

A defensive Dad says, "NORMALLY, I don't do this; and USUALLY, I would let them in, but these idiots should know THAT. LANE. ENDS. RIGHT. THERE!"

Our Dad likes to point when he is mad. The more animated and pointier he gets, the more fear he thinks he puts into those bandits who try to steal his lane.

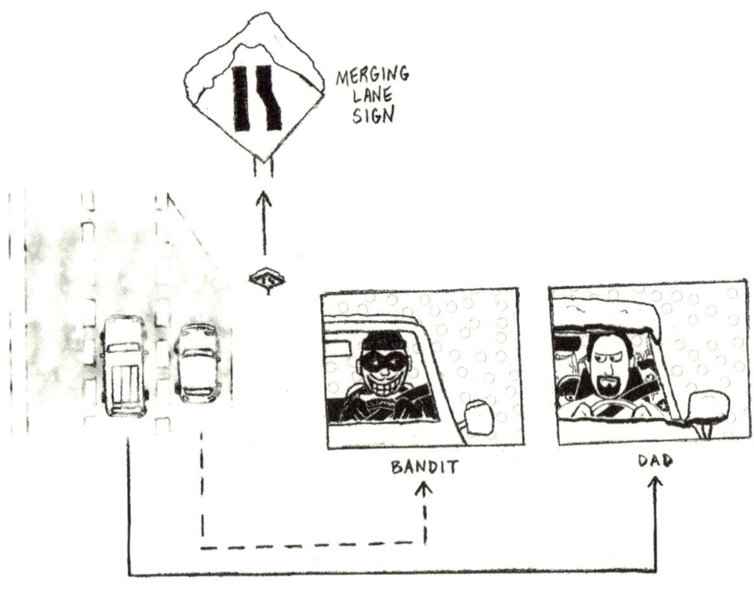

I think Dad unknowingly just growled at this guy, which to me is a little bothersome.

Poor Gertrude always closes her eyes, puts her hands together and prays from the back seat when

Dad drives all crazy like this.

His driving scares her. And her cries used to calm our Dad down to where he would stop; but now, he has grown immune to her weeping, as he tells her that THIS guy just cut him off!

I don't know if this is stereotypical of road raged people or not, but as soon as the person who cut my Dad off gets in front of him our Dad turns into a cop.

Just to put a little more fear into the person who did this despicable act, he always takes off the garage door remote from the sun visor and uses it as a pretend walkie-talkie.

He says, "Breaker breaker 9 over 49er, come in, over." (A legit pause happens here.) "Dispatch, come in, over? Dispatch, are you there, over?"

Gertrude, still in her curled-up position, starts

a "WEE WOO WEE WOO WEE WOO" police siren sound...just for added effect. At least it's keeping her mind off of our Dad's crazy driving.

He is going to keep doing this until one of us responds back, so Luther genuinely cooperates with a "Go for dispatch, over!"

Officer dad explains, "Yeah, we have a situation right now as we head east bound on 87th just past Harlem. Some PICKLE TIP just purposely cut me off, and it's THIS. GUY. RIGHT. HERE!"

Dad even points and waves again to the guy in front of us, so that this bandit can see that Dad is talking about him on his garage door remote...I mean, his walkie-talkie.

Luther happily yells out: "I think we got him, Pa. I can tell by the way he is driving that he thinks you are calling him into the station. I think you got him. Ain't nobody going to mess with us cause we're part of the PO-PO!

"Let's run his plate number, Dad. Here, I'll read it out to you, so you can concentrate on driving.

"B as in bananas...

"M as in Massachewtsits...

"W as in Wabbit...

"7 as in 11...

"H as in Hippo...

"A as in Appotomus...

"W as in Worstchestershire...

"B as in Booooooooo!...

"C as in Conscientious...

"H as in Height or Width...

"L as in L, M, N, O, P...

"S as in Snuck...like this guy just snuck in front of you...

"AAANNNDDD 1!"

I don't know what's worse: The fact that Luther just read out some license plate number without even looking at the guy's license plate or that Dad actually repeated everything Luther said into the garage door remote.

? BMW7HAWBCHLS1

"Oh, we've got this guy now," I communicate to them. "If he can't tell that you're a cop by clearly seeing that you are talking into your garage door remote and that you have your deputy son calling in his European license plate number, while noticing the rest of the family and Grandma are locked up in the back in the station wagon with all these groceries, well, then he is just a stupid dummy!"

Dad tells me that he is "not an on-duty cop"; he is an "off-duty cop."

Makes A LOT more sense now! Kind of like that "six and a half of a dozen of a half of another half of a dozen" saying.

He's a plumber, and I guess he is now an off-duty cop as well!

I'm so proud of him!

My Dad "Doesn't usually do this" but right now he is tailgating this guy just to teach him a lesson!

Dad is tailgating really well, and even Gertrude's crying won't break Dad from the tailgating zone he is in.

Tailgating someone without hitting him or her is one of those skills my Dad has, but tailgating while fishtailing in the snow is more than a skill, it's an art.

Cool! We're even going sideways, and we're still right on this guy without touching his car. Such gracefulness.

If there were paintbrushes on the front bumper of our car and a big piece of canvas on the rear bumper of that guy's car, it would be very interesting to see the masterpiece our Dad would be creating.

Maybe he wants to write a message, like:

"Merry Christmas and please be more careful next time."

Or

"Milk is on sale: $1.99 a gallon at the Yellow Store."

Or

Maybe it would be a drawing of a snowman waving "Hi" to everyone.

Knowing our Dad, the snowman would be waving "Hi" while holding up his carrot in an obscene gesture kind of way!

Luckily, the guy who Dad is tailgating lives right across the street from us. And when I say luckily, I mean unfortunately because Giant Skalinski (who is the largest human being on Earth) looks like a guy who can make our Dad tap out instantly with some MBA submission move.

We pull up to our house and he pulls up to his. They meet in the middle of the street and start "jawing" at each other.

The showdown begins!

Dad keeps mentioning to Giant Skalinski that, "You knew dang well that THAT right lane ends and merges into one lane! You don't belong on the streets if you can't drive like a normal human being!"

Our Dad says a whole bunch of other "kind" things to this man, and when I say kind, I really mean HORRIBLE!

Giant Skalinski keeps telling Dad that he is "very fortunate that tomorrow is Christmas; otherwise, he would make him "eat" every word he just said!"

Ewwwwww, we have two alpha males pumping their chests out, trying to act all alpha-ish. Very vulgar language coming from both of them, and they don't even care that there are children living around these here parts.

When one is done yelling at the other, there is a pause and then we hear the yelling again because we live in a very echo-ish area. Whatever they are saying echoes throughout our neighborhood.

We hear all the vulgar language over and over. And I might add, the acoustics are top notch! Makes me want to start yodeling right here, right now.

To stop this, I can either start a yodel battle, or I am this close to getting out one of those steel chairs and hitting one of them over the head.

Preferably, I would hit Giant Skalinski over the head with the chair, BUT I could turn bad and hit our Dad over the head, just to shock everyone!

Neighbors and fans everywhere would have their mouths wide open and slowly look at each other in amazement!

Nobody would see it coming!

With excitement, I head inside to grab a chair, but then I stop when I realize that thought was a little too extreme. I yell out for Dad to "just give Giant Skalinski some Peacetime." Dad SCREAMS OUT, "Now is not an appropriate time to give anyone some FREAKIN' PEACETIME!"...peacetime... peacetime...peacetime. Beautiful echo right there!

I've about had it with these two. "Hey, hey, hey, hey, hey, hey, hey, hey, hey, hey, hey, hey, hey, hey, hey, hey, hey, hey! Fellas! Really? Some friendly advice from your friendly neighborhood Peacemaker, for the both of you—just keep in mind the almighty Santa is still watching."

All they can do is look at me like a couple of guilty puppies that just got caught tearing up the couch, the love seat, and the recliner.

I yodeled out, "That's it! I'm outta here. I'm going back to the crib!" Petunia yells out from the front porch, "It's not a crib, it's a house. Stop trying to be all cool and everything!"

I would have gotten her with that snowball if she hadn't closed the screen door in time.

CECIL'S SNOWMAN

Walking over to open Grandma Bertha's door, I can't help but laugh at her for a solid two minutes as she is all pressed up against the window.

She is either frozen; or she just can't move.

I can tell I did a great job packing all the grocery bags in tight, as her face is forced hard up against the glass.

I see drool running down the window, and...Oh God! Her dentures are where her eyes are, and her glasses are by her mustache.

She mumbles something about the "Dumb Duck" should get her out of here. Instead, this "Dumb Duck" takes some pictures to capture the moment.

THIS…is money right here!

THIS picture will be on our Christmas cards next year!

How was I to know that when I opened up the car door Grandma would fall out, and the groceries would come tumbling afterwards?

How was I to know that I was supposed to pick up Grandma BEFORE I brought in all of the groceries?

Dad was LIVID both at Giant Skalinski and the fact that Grandma was rolling around in the snow. He tells me that she is NOT making snow angels, and that she needs help getting up because of her bad hip, and THAT SHE IS 71 YEARS OLD!

I'm in shock!

Grandma Bertha is 71 years old? WOW! All this time I thought she was in her 90's—like, upper 90's!

I ask her to hold on a second, as I walk up to her. I

put my arm around her and ask her to turn around.

Selfie time...YES! NAILED IT!

That's probably the best selfie ever. It is Grandma Bertha's face covered in snow with me smiling from ear to ear. Topping off this perfect portrait is the McStup Family Christmas star that is all lit up on the top of our house!

And suddenly, I now have 2 Christmas card cover options!

Our giant star has been a family tradition for years. Dad "FOUND" this star just "LYING" around at his job site, so he has been "PERMANENTLY BORROWING" it for the last few years.

The star is too heavy for our tree outside and it's way too big to go anywhere inside. The first year we had the star it was right here in the middle of the yard—and as Baby Beulah said, "OMG, y'all! That star is like so outta place."

Side note: Baby Beulah is just a toddler, but she has recently developed this valley girl/hillbilly language, and we have no idea where it came from.

Can you guess who came up with the idea of moving the star to the top of the house? That's right, THIS GUY! (Me)

People love that star and come from all over just to see it. I feel like a celebrity and I purposely stand outside freezing my butt off just so I can be included in the people's pictures.

As Grandma Bertha is walking up towards the house, with her face still full of snow and little boogie icicles, she notices the newly created snowman in our front yard.

Grandma is BLUNT and does not care what she says about anything or anyone. That is definitely her top weakness.

She stops and stares at this unusual looking snowman. She can't help but get her 2 cents in, as she blurts out, "THAT is the WORST snowman I have EVER..." That's when Cecil emerges out from inside the snowman and tells Grandma Bertha to stop and think about the Mother Ducky consequences before she says anything bad about his "Fabulous the Snowman"! Grandma just grasps her heart, as she slowly falls to her knees in shock!

After helping Grandma up AGAIN, Dad becomes even more LIVID.

Side note: Livid is way madder than just plain old mad. It's at the very end of the mad meter!

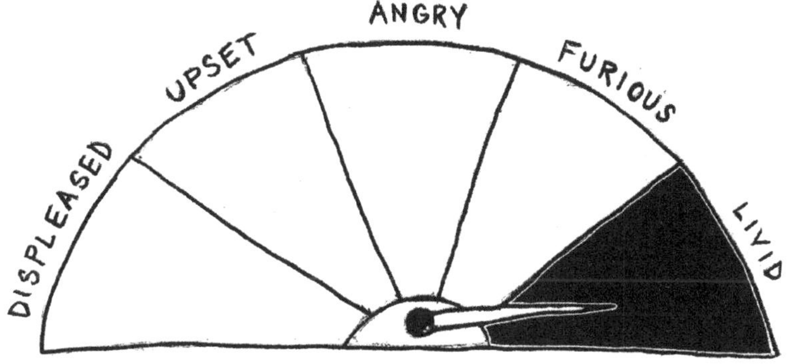

Dad is now ruffing and scruffing all the way up the stairs. I notice his sour mood, so I become kind and hold the door open for him. As he walks on past me, I gently whisper to him "ladies first" and give a quick giggle. He doesn't find it as amusing as I do.

Then, I cut quickly in front of Grandma Bertha and let the door close on her because I ain't holding any doors for her since she's not a lady!

Finally, these last few hours are over and Dad can relax before he has a nervous breakdown. Maybe he can drink his good old spiked eggnog...but that's when Mom comes walking by!

THE CHRISTMAS TREE

Our Mom interrupts Dad talking to himself and says, "Elmer! Where's the Turkey?"

As she is comparing the list and the receipt, she yells, "There are a few things from the list that I didn't come across that are not listed on this receipt! Did you forget to get the Turkey and the Ham?"

Dad says, "Heck no Maude! I got the darn turkey and the dang ham!"

Dad storms into the kitchen and opens the refrigerator. He takes out the deli turkey and then slams the door closed! He comes right back into the front room and shows her that turkey! He then tells her that he also got the ham, but HER son ate the dang ham while we were in the checkout line!

Side note: Dad and Mom use the old "HER" son or "HER" daughter or "HIS" son or "HIS" daughter...A LOT! Mostly, this kind of talk happens when we do something wrong and they suddenly don't want to claim us. This talk always confuses me! I never know if I am only HIS son or HER son. They say this for each and every one of us kids—like some big twist in a movie. It makes me wonder.

Is he my real dad?

Pa Pa?

Is that woman actually my mommy?

Are these my actual Brothers and Sisters or just some kids they found on the streets?

Anyway, in Dad's defense, he almost always gets deli turkey and deli ham.

In Mom's defense, she wrote down a 16 lb turkey and a 10 lb ham on that shopping list.

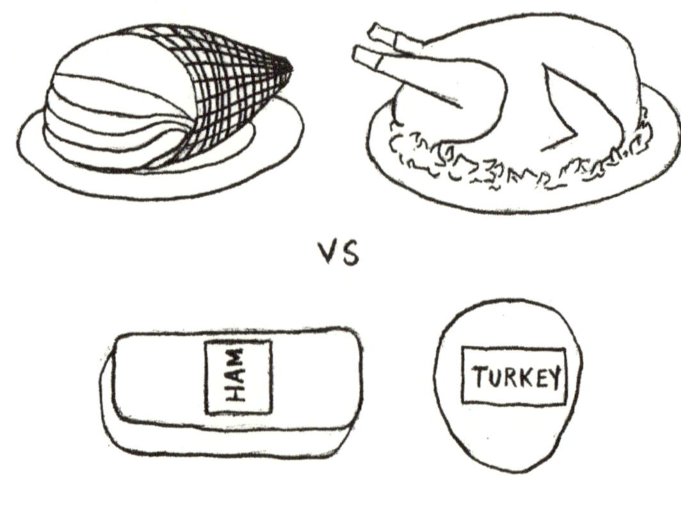

In Dad's defense, he thought it was 1.6 lbs of turkey (which seems a little odd) and 1.0 lb of ham.

He even took the list out of her hand to show her exactly what she wrote down. "I could have SWORN there was a DECIMAL POINT between the 1 and the 6 and between the 1 and the 0," he shouted!

Mom starts laughing and laughing until Dad accuses her of erasing those decimal points!

OH MAN, now Mom is verbally giving it to him. I ask her if she wants a steel chair, but she is too focused on her clever Rated PG swear word sayings: She shouts, "BOLOGNA FOOEY!" She calls him a "JIVE BUTT TURKEY", while telling him to "suck an egg" and that he is in "deep doo-doo!"

In shock, I ask her if she kisses her husband with that potty mouth.

While the tirade goes on, Dad just holds his head down in shame. By the way, this would have been the ideal time to hit him over the head with a steel chair!

A suddenly nicer, gentler Dad arises and apologizes.

He also confesses that he wasn't able to locate the Croy Sants.

"The what?" our Mom asks.

"The Croy Sants," our Dad explains.

Confused our Mom asks again, "Our what?"

Dad is becoming more frustrated as he yells out, "The Croy Sants! The CROY SANTS! The DARN CROY SANTS. They don't have any of the blasted CROY SANTS!"

I interrupt and ask him if he could use it in a sentence.

A confused Mom asks, "What in tarnation is a CROY SANT?"

Dad is getting even more frustrated saying, "A Croy...SANT!"

I interrupt again and ask him if he could tell us the origin.

Dad explains, "Maude, they are the things you like instead of dinner rolls!"

Mom gives him a blank stare.

Dad continues, "You really have no idea what they're called? You put butter on them. I even asked this young kid, who worked there, if they had any Croy Sants and the kid just looked at me like I was an idiot!"

Luther blurts out, "Kind of like how Mom is looking at you right now?"

Dad slowly turns and looks at Luther.

I told Dad: "Na ah, Nope. The focus is not on Luther right now. This is between you and your wife!" Then, I point to the both of them.

A little silence and then it dawns on our Mom that the magic word our Dad is trying to say is... croissants! She can tell that Dad is struggling, so she just takes out a pen and paper and starts writing. That was very kindhearted of Mom because all she wants for Christmas is for Dad to NOT give himself a heart attack!

She calmly makes him another list. The list is short and only has a few items on it...BUT GOD HELP HIM if he messes THIS list up! He might as well pack his bags and head for the hills!

The "WHY DAD HAS TO GO BACK TO THE STORE" list:

*1 regular 16 LB TURKEY (Not sliced deli Turkey)

*1 regular 10 LB HAM (Not sliced deli Ham)

*CROISSANTS (NOT CROY SANTS)

I tell him, "By the way, I saw a sign by the croissants that said: 'Buy one, get one half off!' So, make sure you pile up on them! I love me some good croissants!"

In disbelief, Mad Dad asks, "You saw the croissants, and you didn't say anything to me about them?"

I say, "I didn't realize you were looking for croissants. I thought you were looking for some Croy Sants. And I did not know what that was, otherwise..."

He interrupts me and tells me to just shut up. So, I do.

Returning to the "WHY DAD HAS TO GO BACK TO THE STORE" list:

*Redeem all of those coupons that you forgot to redeem

*Return the EARS of corn and get CANS of corn

*Get non-smooshed hot dog buns

*Get a carton of non-cracked eggs

*Get non-flattened bread

I tell him he might as well go back to the burger joint and get his 3 cents back while he is out and about.

An agitated Mom asks, "What 3 cents?"

Grandma rolls her eyes and says, "Good Lord, here we go!"

That's when a magical puff of steam comes from the top of our Dad's head.

I should just shut up. Why did I say that? I meant, no harm. Sometimes I just blurt out stuff that I shouldn't blurt out. Give me a piece of dang duct tape, so I can put it over my mouth!

I feel shame, so I say, "Petunia, go get me a piece of duct tape, so I can put it over my mouth!" She seemed eager and RAN into the garage to tear me off a piece of duct tape.

Before I put that tape over my mouth, I want our Mom to know that our Dad did indeed ask for the 3 pennies back. I ask Mom to guess what the cashier lady had the gall to say back to dad.

Mom turns to me and firmly says, "WHAT?"

Overjoyed, I say, "Grandma Bertha has a big butt! How would the cashier lady even know that?"

No reaction at all. Everyone is so serious around these here parts.

Mom insists on Dad going back now and getting those 3 cents.

Dad vows he is not going back just to get 3 dang pennies.

They went back and forth until my Mom says, "FINE! I'll just walk there and get the 3 cents back!"

She stands up and heads towards the front door in her bare feet and without a coat or hat.

She begins mumbling about feeling lightheaded and that she feels like she might pass out; she has to sit back down.

Side note: Real or not, our Mom always faints. It's a great tool she uses when we act up or when things are not going her way—just one of her many strengths.

The threat of Mom going outside in the blizzard (with no coat or shoes on) just to get 3 cents back at a place that was over a mile away is entertaining; however, she knows that Dad would never let her do it, so he caves.

As a peace offering, I give Baby Beulah my pillow with 3 pennies on it to take over to Dad.

I wink and nod at him, giving him the "I got your back" signal.

He swipes those 3 pennies and the pillow.

I am proud to announce that I come fully equipped with SUPERPOWERS!

One of those superpowers is I can sense when something is about to happen, like right now when Dad starts his windup and is about to whip that peace offering pillow right back at me.

Being all quick and everything, I reach for Petunia and pull her...by her hair, to shield me from the oncoming pillow.

A direct hit to her heart! I can't understand why she is all mad. She was right next to me and I couldn't help my reactions.

If anything, she should be appalled at our Dad for throwing that 90 MPH fastball pillow at her heart. Quit holding your heart, it was a dang pillow that hit you! You're lucky it wasn't a wooden steak, or a silver bullet, or a bucket of water because you would certainly be a goner if any of those 3 things hit you!

Since Mom saw him take the peace offering pennies, she says he better not even think about using ANY OTHER 3 pennies, if he knows what is good for him.

Dad just scowls at the Christmas tree, as he mumbles that he needs a drink.

Mom says, "NO! What you need to do is go back and get a flipping 16 LB Turkey, a 10 LB Ham, croissants, cans of corn, bread, buns, eggs and to redeem those coupons!"

I remove the duct tape and remind him about the 3 cents, only because I am worried about his well-being if he forgets.

His glare at the Christmas tree got REAL!

Whatever Mom is yelling right now is just mumbo jumbo to him. Her words are not getting past that force field surrounding Dad's ears.

His feet move back and forth and back and forth, as he stares down this 7-foot tall Douglas fir tree.

Dad begins puffing like a Bull. His head and eyebrows tilt downwards, while his teeth are like magnets, as they bond to each other.

Heavily breathing through the cracks of those

teeth, he starts muttering some words. I think he is speaking in Latin or something.

And then it happens.

His teeth demagnetize as he releases the ultimate, "MOTHER!!!"

He begins spreading his arms wide open and then, suddenly, he charges the tree!

All of his pent-up anger and aggression is about to be released onto this defenseless, well lit, but poorly decorated tree!

He jumps and gives the tree this bear hug, spear tackle. At the same time, he turns his body, knowing he is going out the window with the tree in his arms!

Side note: We used to have a double pane glass picture window, but a few years ago, a big summer storm blew the single pane right out and into the front yard, leaving one pane of glass. The house is so old that the frame around the window was rotting away, and the caulk was peeling off. Barely any wood was holding the window in place.

I wish he would have let us know he was going to do this amazing stunt, so I could have recorded it. He went through that window so gracefully and as perfectly as anyone could possibly go out a picture window.

I'm not usually easily impressed, but right now, I am...easily impressed!

Petunia tells us that it's a good thing that the glass hit the soft snow-filled bushes. Thankfully, the window kind of stuck there and created a slanted slope that allowed Dad and the tree to slide down at the same time.

All of us just stood there, in shock, silently watching the snow come into the front room.

After hearing a knock on the door, Ernie nervously asks, "Who could that be?" as he ran off to hide.

Side note: No stranger has entered our house in years. This is because of the horrible condition that it's in. If we hear a doorbell or a knock...we run!

Gertrude opens the door, and in comes a happy Dad walking backwards followed by the Christmas tree, which had bumps and bruises along with broken branches. I think Dad is ecstatic because he knows the window didn't break, and he just got away with a Christmas miracle!

He puts the tree right back where it originally was—LIKE. NOTHING. EVER. HAPPENED.

In a stunned silence, Cecil whispers "ABERA... CA...DABERA!"

At the same time, Ernie whispers, "ALA...KA...BAMA!"

That was quite amazing, but to me something else happened that was equally as incredible. There is a very special ornament that our Mom made in memory of our late sister, Lilly. Each and every year we put Lilly's ornament right in the middle of our Christmas tree.

Even though Lilly is not here with us physically, we feel like she is still here with us in spirit. Literally, there are things that have happened that make us think that she is still here with us. We will save that story for another time.

When our Dad tackled the tree and it went out the window, Lilly's ornament flew off the tree and landed in our Mom's lap. It was miraculous because she was sitting in the opposite direction and a good 10 ft away from where the tree was.

The tree is broken, but it looks cool now. A few of the broken branches look like arms. Most of the lights are not working now, but the ones that do, make the tree glow. The remaining working lights form a mouth while the unbroken ornaments create the eyes and nose. We give the tree a bow tie with the salvaged garland.

With some tweaking here and there, we have a grand, brand new, Christmas tree. Our tree just went through a major transformation in a matter of minutes!

It is a tradition of ours to name our Christmas trees after family and friends. And so, without any further ado, ladies and gentlemen, I present to you our NEW Christmas tree...Jimmy Jo!

STOCKINGS

Every Christmas Eve, sometime before bedtime, all of us lay out our stockings on one of the couches in the front room. We put the stockings on the couch, basically, because there is no other place that can hold all 8 of them. We don't really have "STOCKINGS" per say. We just use good old regular socks, which is fine, because it does the same job as a fancy schmancy stocking.

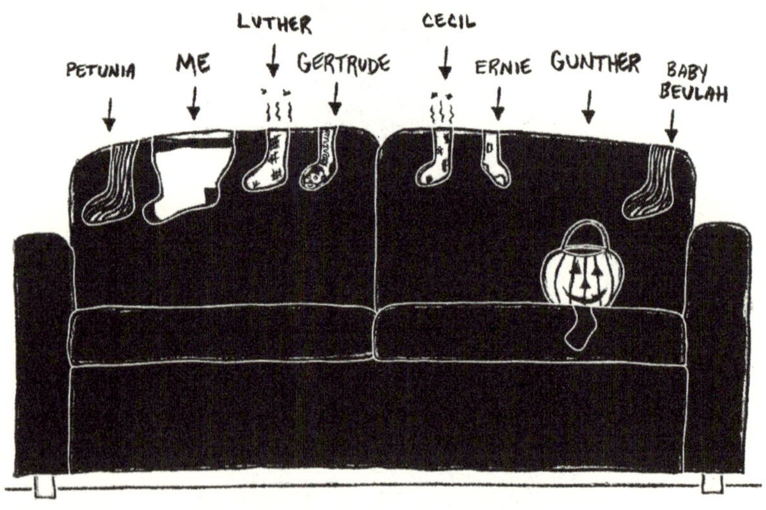

Petunia always lends Baby Beulah one of her socks; otherwise, Beulah would get screwed because obviously her little toddler socks can't hold that much.

Gertrude, by far, has the nicest sock out there—all decorated with a googly eyed Santa, and she even went so far as having her name stitched onto it.

As for me, I always stretch the fudge out of my sock, just to gain more room in there. I mean, I take a sock a few days before Christmas and I sit there for hours just stretching it out ANNND stretching it out, just like taffy. I don't even know how I did it, but I can now fit my entire head into my sock!

Technically, at one point in time, ALL the brothers' socks that are up there, used to be my socks. They're hand-me-down socks...to the 5th power! I don't know...it's kind of cool. Makes me feel like I'm helping them out in a special giving kind of way!

Someone should really tell Ernie that he should choose a sock WITHOUT holes. He might get lucky if Santa puts an Orange or an Apple in the sock first. That would seal off the hole and prevent anything small from falling out of it.

Gunther doesn't mess around, as he always puts his Halloween trick or treat plastic pumpkin out. He is so smart. You see, he rigged the pumpkin by putting a hole on the bottom of it. Then, he taped the opening of the sock to that hole on his pumpkin. Technically, I guess, it is still a stocking.

Lastly but not leastly, we have Cecil's and Luther's socks. God love them! They just take a sock directly off their foot and use it. That's their tradition. They've been doing this for years. This would be somewhat acceptable if it wasn't for the fact that they don't change out their socks for days! Plus, the socks smell like corn chips—on a good day. It either gags you or makes you hungry, depending on how hungry you are.

THE CAROLERS

Christmas Eve excitement is building, and there is still time before we have to go to bed for the night. I decide to gather up my brothers and run a little idea past them that just came to me.

What if we do a spur of the moment, neighborhood Christmas Carol Concert?

We can go door to door and just sing our guts out!

Individually, we can't sing to save your life. Put us together and somehow...never mind, we're even worse! We really can't sing, but we sure can make up for that with our boy band good looks and our flailing arms, legs and hip dance maneuvers!

Plus, we could sing some of Cecil's super songs that he has put a lot of time and effort into creating.

The brothers are alllll in!

We're ready to head outside to our first house!

Wait; before we head out, we need some of those FLICKERING candles!

Darn it! We don't have any FLICKERING candles. We need something to illuminate our path. Luther's idea of using homemade torches probably won't work...only because I'm sure Dad and Mom will have 'some kind of problem with it.'

Flashlights will have to do!

It's snowing and it's freezing, so we bundle up quickly, throwing on some coats, ski masks and gloves.

We quietly break out of our house and head over towards the next block.

We chose that area as our starting point because the houses over there are way bigger. And we figure, the bigger the house, the bigger the tips!

We arrive at the Jordan's house. This is one of the biggest homes in our area.

All the brothers are a little nervous and a little giddy right now, as we relentlessly ring the first doorbell.

Some grumpy looking guy opens the door, and that's our cue to begin.

We're two minutes into our caroling and Cecil begins yelling, "SSSSSTOP, just SSSSSTOP! Look we're all doing a fabulous job, but we're just not in sync with each other. Also, nobody is putting his or her hearts into this. It's about feelings, people.

They need to feel us, and we need to feel them! These people can tell when we mean it and when we are just trying to make a dollar."

He's absolutely right, so we up our entire game!

Still, we are not getting the reaction that we were expecting! All we're getting are weird stares. Halfway through our performance, Mr. Jordan just abandoned us. It's as if we are some peanut shells that people just throw on the floor at a restaurant!

House after house and person after person, the same thing keeps happening.

These peanut shell-throwing people open the door, stare at us for a minute or so and then slam the door closed. It's like they saw a ghost or something.

And, it looks like everyone has been sleeping. What is everybody, old? This is odd, but okay, we'll deal with it.

We move on to the next house. Again, we psych ourselves up for our neighborhood Christmas Carol Concert.

Cecil wants us to be more "theatrical" this time. It should make up for everything else that we are lacking.

These are Cecil's songs. He wrote all the lyrics, so we know it has to be good! It would mean a lot to him if someone just told him how good these songs are.

We ring the doorbell to Mrs. Payton's place, and as soon as she opens her door, we begin.

Ernie hits the play button on his phone, so we can have some background music; and one by one, we shine our flashlights onto our ski masks.

Then, we gently sing in harmony...

♫♪ "OH MY GOODNESS,
WHAT ARE WE DOING HERE?
YOU REALLY DON'T KNOW US,
AND WE REALLY DON'T CARE!
WE WANT YOUR MONEY,
AND DEMAND YOUR LOVE!
SO, BREAK YOUR PIGGY BANK,
OR YOU MIGHT GET SHOVED!
WE'RE GOING TO SING AND DANCE,
SO SIT RIGHT DOWN.
DON'T YOU SHUT THAT DOOR,
'CAUSE THAT WILL MAKE US FROWN!" ♪♫

Coincidently, this is where she attempts to shut the door. Luckily, Gunther gets part of his foot and thigh in there before it closes all the way. A frantic Cecil yells, "Pick up the pace! We have to pick up the pace, people!"

We continue:
♫♪ "YO!
SANTA'S IN ATLANTA, THEN OFF TO MONTANA.
BACK TO LOUISIANA, BEFORE HE HITS INDIANA.
HE'S ZIGZAGGING ALL OVER THE PLACE,
JUST SO HE CAN SEE
EACH & EVERYBODY'S FACE." ♪♫

Even though he is biting and scratching, Gunther

is slowly losing his battle to keep the door from closing.

Our goal right now is to just complete a dang song before anyone closes a door on us.

We're getting close.

Luther tells him, "C'mon Gunther! Don't worry about her foot in your face."

Speed round:
♫♪ "SANTA, IS THE COMMAND–AHH
WHO BEGAN–AHH
CHRISTMAS PLAN–AHH.
BRINGING GIFTS FOR KIDS LIKE
AMANDA
AND SUSANNA,
AND EVEN SOME FOR COUSIN JEBIDIAH.
NOW DON'T SAY HE CAN'T–AHH
GIVE A PANDA
A BANANA
THAT'S VERY, VERY TANTA...LIZING
AND SURPRISING!" ♪♫

Ernie takes over:
♫♪ "CAUSE HE COULDA WOULDA SHOULDA,
AND SHOULDA WOULDA COULDA,

AND COULDA WOULDA SHOULDA,
AND SHOULDA WOULDA COULDA.
WOULDA.
SHOULDA.
COULDA." ♪♫

Our hearts break as Mrs. Payton hits Gunther with a broom, breaking his hold on the door.

We were sooo close. Only five more minutes and we would have been done! A defeated Cecil says, "Guys, we should just give up. Maybe Christmas caroling is not our thing."

But, wait!

It's not all bad news, though, because...who is that peeking out from her window curtains? Why, that is Mrs. Payton peeking out. Clearly, she is on the phone with somebody.

A confused Ernie says, "I have this feeling that she is on the phone with someone from HOLLYWOOD, CALIFORNIA!"

Cecil excitedly shouts, "Yes! Yes! Oh...My...Gosh! Yes! Ernie, you are right! This is our big break. It all starts by word of mouth. Peeking Payton is now a friend and possible ally. It all starts right here, right now! The show must go on!"

The brothers become super giddy, as we convince ourselves that Mrs. Payton is calling the Hollywood agents, or the paparazzi, or some people like that!

Possible fame will not stop us, though! Cecil wants us to continue and finish the entire song for our loyal fan.

Peeking Payton is still watching us.

I'm pointing at her and then I point to the door because I think she can hear us much, much better if she is outside instead of listening to us from the inside.

Anyway, after we are done singing, we go back up to the door, and we ask if we can have some money.

ANY MONEY? You know, a tip.

That is the only reason why we are doing this thing at 10:00 at night in the first place. So, we can make a little something-something!

But Mrs. Payton, just like everyone else, starts screaming when we ask for any money.

Why?

I've never seen anybody scream at someone when they ask for a tip?

Maybe, she doesn't realize who we are? So, we run over to the window and start pulling up our ski masks, while shining the flashlights directly into our faces.

I say, "Look, it's me! It's me!"

These ski masks are hard to pull over your face when you're holding a flashlight and your hands are freezing!

Mrs. Payton screamed so loud that not one of us was able to fully get our ski masks off, so we quickly put them back on and swiftly walk away!

Luther doesn't think she saw any of our faces, and he doesn't want to lose her as a potential customer. So, as we run, he looks back and yells out, "Did you see any of our faces? Do you know any of us? We will be back in the next few days to show you who we are—and that's a promise!"

As we run, Luther reminds us that we don't want to let her down!

We try a different block now, and Cecil suggests we try something different this time.

One of Cecil's famous sayings is KISS! A.K.A. "Keep It Simple, Silly!"

Great idea! We will follow Cecil's advice.

I know this next house; a single mom and her 3 kids live here. Really nice, caring AND giving woman! We see them from a distance every Sunday at church, so I think our luck will change right now.

We don't need our flashlights for this one because this house is near a streetlight. So, to give a little more drama to our new performance, Cecil instructs the brothers to keep their jazz fingers pointed in their coat pockets.

After pounding on her door for quite a while, she finally opens it, and we start our performance by singing about some of our friends:

♫♪ "WELL, THERE'S ROCKY AND BOBBY AND VINNIE

AND VITO...LOUIE AND JOEY AND FRANKIE AND GUIDO. BUT, CAN ANYONE RECALLLLL, WHO IS OUR BEST FRIEND OF THEM ALLLLL?" ♪♫

Side note: This lady has no clue!

We continue singing:
♫♪ "ANTHONY THE RED-HEADED TONYYYY, HAS A VERY RED-HEADED...HEAD. AND, IF YOU EVER SAW HIMMMM...YOU WOULD EVEN SAY IT'S...RED!" ♪♫

Side note: Cecil has some strong lyric writing skills!

The single mom closes the door, yet she still seems fascinated enough to watch us through her window!

Still in sync, we continue:
♫♪ "ALL OF OUR OTHER FRIENDS, USED TO GIGGLE AND CALL HIM NAMES, LIKE: 'FRECKLE HEAD' OR 'TOMATO PASTE' OR 'PIMPLE RED' OR 'FANCY FACE...'" ♪♫

I excitedly add, "And, I really hope you give us some money, lady!" (I kind of went off script there.)

Anyway, Cecil is about to get a little bit more in depth regarding what our friends were all about!

And now, it's time for Cecil's sassy solo.

But...instead of singing, Cecil suddenly goes off on a rant as he exclaims: "These guys had the nerve to tell Anthony the red-headed Tony that he should 'Go see a hairstylist' or 'Just cover that thing up with a wig.' Some of them even said, 'You should go to a nicer department store somewhere downtown, and you should probably purchase yourself some extensions, honey!'"

Cecil surprised all of us by going off script. There's some awkward silence and a whole lot of staring at Cecil going on...because that had nothing to do with nothing right there.

Cecil composes himself and reminds us that we should get visibly upset and even more theatrical because this is the part where the friends are not letting poor Tony join in ANY of their backyard games.

Ernie suddenly yells, "Owwwww!! Gunther, stop it!" Gunther is being a little too theatrical, as he karate chops the air and then accidentally kicks Ernie with one of his leg extension kicks.

Luther slowly walks up to her window, stares in

and says, "These pals of ours would even say, 'I swear to Santa, I DOUBLE DOG DIPPITY DARE you to touch my bocce balls; I dare you!'"

Side note: This lady is really into the story right now because her eyes are the size of two pizza pies.

Luther continues telling her about how there was some fog on that Christmas Eve.

Side note: For added effects, Cecil, Ernie, Gunther and I stand next to Luther and do some heavy breathing so you can see our breath in the cold.

Surrounded by breath-fog, Luther continues: "Out from the fog, Anthony, the red-headed Tony, walked right up to the others with what appeared to be a squirt gun of some sorts."

Cecil jumps in and dramatically blurts out: "Anthony then told our other friends, ' Look, you sons of guns! I'm not cutting these lava-flowing, red locks for anyone OR anything. And you guys better BACK OFF! Ya see!'"

All the brothers join together in singing for the grand finale:
♫♪ "THEN, HOW ALL OF THESE FRIENDS (SUDDENLY AND FUNNILY) LOVED HIM, AS THEY SHOUTED OUT WITH SOME OF THIS GLEEEEE: ' ANTHONY, THE RED-HEADED TONYYYY, CAN WE PLEASE MAKE YOU SOME SPAAAA-GHETTIIII?'" ♪♫

By far, this was our best performance yet! Wait... where did the single mom go?

We stop, smile and just stare at her house. All of us look up, down, left and right at every nook and cranny of her house.

After gawking for a solid minute or two, looking for any movement, finally the door opens...AND

OUT COMES THE MONEY!

This lady must have been so impressed because she just gave us a $500 tip!!

She's obviously so starstruck because you can see her shaking. She said she would have given us EVEN MORE money, but there was no more left to give.

JACKPOT!

This made up for all the time we spent busting our behinds off trying to make an honest dollar!

Fist pumps, chest bumps, hugs and high fives are flying around everywhere!

Then, we take our closing bows to show appreciation to this kindhearted woman whom we now call...our greatest fan! We are ecstatic, as we end our neighborhood Christmas Carol Concert on a high note!

$500 for the 5 of us to split!

Now, I just have to figure out how to divide this up between all of us. It's going to be hard trying to explain why I think I should get $300 of the $500, but I think I can convince most of them! Let's see, when you add the bonuses, take out the taxes, factor in the deductable, and carry the two...yeah, I think I can talk them into it.

Heading back home, we notice a few cop cars are parked in front of our house. My heart starts POUNDING, as I get that sick to my stomach feeling.

I just know, deep down inside that one of these things must have just happened...

1) Someone was robbed or mugged!

2) Some sort of escape room murder mystery thing has just taken place...and nobody could escape!

Or worst of all...OH GOD!

3) Somebody has kidnapped Gunther!!

This has been a horrible fear of mine for some time now.

Ewww, these sick people who took him played it so well, waiting until Christmas Eve when nobody would expect it. I can see them planning it on a lesser holiday like Groundhog Day or Cyber Friday... but now? Too clever!

Obviously, it had to be one of these three circumstances that happened. The cops have never really been to our house, so why are they here now?

I tell the brothers to "come on", as we run towards our house. We are shaking right now. That's how nervous we are!

Returning to our yard, we hop the fence...some more gracefully than others.

We approach our parents and see our mom crying as they talk to the police officers. Our Mom is overjoyed to see us, as she thanks God over and over that we are all fine!

But, that happiness quickly goes away when I ask her if she saw Gunther anywhere.

Visibly shaken, she said, "No! Isn't he with you guys?"

All I could do is envision him putting up a great fight, as they took him away. I sadly tell her, "They got him, ma. They got him."

I slope down towards the step as I sit in shock.

Our Mom says that she is going to faint, but before she plops down right where she is, our Dad says, "Wait a second! Isn't that Gunther right there behind you?"

Sadly, I tell him no, it's just me.

He says, "NO! Not YOU! There! Right there! Isn't that Gunther waving at us? 1-2-3-4-5! There are five of you boys, so that has to be him."

The cop says, "Alright! Everyone take off your ski masks, so we can see who's who!" So, we all go along with it and take them partially off.

As she runs down the steps to hug him, Mom rejoices, "GUNTHER!!!!!!!! Oh, thank the dear Lord! My baby is safe. I'm so glad that you're okay!"

I share in the hug and tell Gunther to never ever let anyone kidnap him EVER AGAIN! Gunther is so confused that all he could do is join us in crying.

Cecil joins the huddle and cries out, "Oh, thank the dear Lord that I am OKAY as well!"

Dad has been silently repeating to Mom that everything is OKAY, but she won't listen to him.

The police start interrogating Luther and Ernie by questioning them and saying that our parents were petrified that something bad had happened to us. They began to worry when all five of us went missing.

Also, combine that with the information that many neighbors called in and reported that there were five lunatics dressed up in ski masks, roaming the neighborhood, singing odd songs, and demanding money.

The cop asked us what in the world were we doing? Luther replied in some southern accent, "There are certain things we don't reveal to the authorities."

Now, WE have some explaining to do!

I explain that WE were bored, and that WE came up with this idea to have a Christmas Carol Concert for all of our neighbors to make them feel some joy.

Plus, WE could make some money off this thing. WE saw some people doing it on TV and thought that WE could do the same thing. That's all.

WE went a little later than normal because WE were smart. WE knew that there wasn't any Christmas Carol Competition at this time of night. So, WE swooped on in. WE had the whole neighborhood to ourselves.

The officer wants more details.

I inform the officer that as we started our performance, three of us would stay in view in front of the doorway, one would hide just to the left of the door, and one would hide just to the right of the door.

Then, when it was the appropriate time in the song, they would jump out for theatrical purposes only!

We sincerely tried to do a great job for everyone!

We wanted to be better than all the other carolers. We wanted it to be memorable. So, we did it like how we did it.

The police officer wanted to know why we didn't let our parents know that we were going to do this. I told him, "It was obvious. It's Christmas Eve and it was around 10:00 pm. Do you really think our parents would let us do this if we asked them?"

The cop brought up that people don't go around caroling to make money; they do it to get people into the Christmas spirit.

Luther says, "Well tell that to the woman who threw $500 at us."

A whole bunch of high fiving, peace timing, and cheering are coming from the brothers; even our parents look kind of pleasantly surprised!

Hold up! What just happened?

Would you believe the head of the po-po made us give the money to him, so he could give it back to the single mom?

Unreal!

Luther is trying to get at him and is growling really loud in his direction.

The cop asks us, "What's the problem here?"
A skeptical Luther says, "Stereotypical BAIT question...COPPER!"

I explain that the problem is this, "You just took our hard earned $500 from us, and now we can't help out our favorite charity, which is F.F.F.F.—and that's on you, son!"

He told me not to call him "son" and wanted to know what the F.F.F.F. is?

Luther tells him, "It's not what you think it is, perv. It stands for FIVE hundred dollars FOR FIVE FELLAS!"

Luther stresses each and every "F" to show importance.

Some awkward silence is going on....

At that very moment, Grandma Bertha dramatically appears at the front door.

Banging on the storm door and looking all scary

with her curlers in her hair...she FRAZZLES all of us big time, which prompts me to go into natural reaction mode.

I put my hands together and make a finger gun with my pointer fingers. I point that PF57 (Pointer finger 57) right at her and start reading Grandma Bertha her rights.

SCREAMING, I yell out, "YOU AND YOUR BIG BUTT HAVE THE RIGHTS TO REMAIN SILENT! NOW REPEAT AFTER ME! I, GRANDMA BERTHA AND MY BIG BUTT, WE DO TOGETHER SOLEMNLY SWEAR TO TELL THE TRUTH, THE WHOLE TRUTH, AND NOTHING BUT THE TRUTH AND FOR THE TRUTH, THE POWER, THE GLORY AND THE JUSTICE AND THE LIBERTY FOR ALL. AND IF YOU DON'T...SO HELP ME GOD... BECAUSE THIS LAND IS MY LAND, AND THIS LAND IS YOUR LAND!"

I don't know the rest of that poem, so I just stop. I am so worked up and shaking so badly that Grandma Bertha is really lucky I don't just accidentally shoot her with my PF57.

Breathing through my nostrils, I lower my pointer fingers. Then, I take one giant step back, as I turn and lower the Billy club that Luther is pointing at Grandma Bertha.

Finally, I gently give the Billy club back to the officer.

My instincts were to read Grandma Bertha her dog gone rights while Luther's instincts was to grab the officer's Billy club. We were in instinct mode and we couldn't contain ourselves!

"Merry Christmas," Luther says to the officer, as he slowly smiles at him.

I don't know. I'm tired and I'm getting anxious, so I just tell mom and dad that they can handle this mess. We are going to bed because Santa is coming soon!

We just walk right in and go to bed, like...nothing... ever...happened!

Luther somehow found "another" $500 just lying on the porch—a true Christmas miracle. What are those odds?

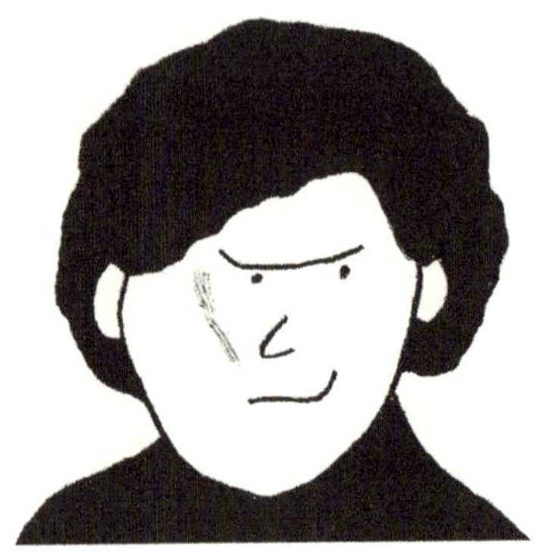

Caroling is not for everyone. I am truly exhausted, as I feel like I ran a marathon, in Chicago or Boston!

This has to be the fastest we have ever gone

to bed. All of us brothers are in bed within 60 seconds of each other!

But before we go to sleep, I must set my alarm clock to exactly 6:55 AM.

That's 6–FIFTY–FIVE!

Shoot...6:57, I went past it.

My mind wanders...I wonder if Santa will have to use our bathroom? #1 or #2?

6:56...DANG IT! I MISSED IT AGAIN.

I can't focus...I like getting up early on Christmas.

6:58...DANG IT! THIS CLOCK IS TOO FAST!

I set my alarm early...6:52...because...6:53... it...6:54...gives me...6:55...an hour to hit snooze...6:56!

SHOOT! THIS IS RIDICULOUS!

You know what? My concentration sucks! The heck with this clock! I'm just going to use my own biology clock and get up by myself.

Some time passes and as the clock gets closer to midnight, I look around at my brothers, and I am amazed that they are all sleeping within minutes of lying down.

HOW DID THEY DO THAT?

Usually, I can't stand it when I can't fall asleep, but to be honest with you, I'm kind of looking forward to some insomnia tonight.

You know, the big man and his reindeer are going to be here tonight, so maybe it's not the worst thing in the world if I'm awake when they arrive.

If I do see him, I'm half debating if I should put on a diaper and just crawl into his bag because I know for a FACT that this has happened before. AND he just let that kid live at the North Pole with him!

Yep! That will be my plan.

But, as I was looking around for a pen and paper to write my farewell letters to the "fam", I suddenly remembered what our Mom and our Dad told us earlier in the day.

Mom told us that we MUST be asleep before the

clock strikes 12 o'clock midnight! She looked super serious, like she was going to start crying as she said, "If there is any child awake at the stroke of midnight then Santa's sleigh turns into a pumpkin, MID FLIGHT, no matter where he is!"

I remember my eyes got REALLY big when Mom said this.

She sounded and looked legitimately worried that we would not go to bed and that we would cause Santa to fall from the sky.

Dad saw Mom stressing out, so he interrupted her and said, "It's a very rare thing, BUT it has happened. It seems to happen once every 34 years, and THIS is the 34th year!"

Then, Dad started freaking me out because he started looking upwards at the ceiling as he TOOOO CALMLY said, "Every 34 years...for 34 days...Santa walks the Earth, searching for the KID who was awake and turned his sleigh into a pumpkin, and made him fall from the sky."

Side note: I don't know why Dad suddenly looked down at me when he screamed out "KID", but he was specifically looking at me!!!

I can't have that on me!

I can't be the one who causes that!

Looking at the clock, I realize I have less than 10

THE END

ABOUT THE AUTHOR

Patrick McErlean has thought about writing books since he was in his 20's. He thought about it even more when he was in his 30's. When he reached his 40's, he seriously thought about it and decided now is the time to start writing. He never gives up! Born and raised in the Southwest suburbs of Chicago, he currently lives in Western Kentucky with his beautiful wife and two beautiful daughters. In his free time, Patrick loves to spend time with his family or watching his favorite Chicago sports teams, The White Sox, Bears, Blackhawks, and Bulls!

ABOUT THE ILLUSTRATOR

Michael McErlean is an experienced graphic designer and now...a professional illustrator! He loves creating art and has done so since his younger days making masterpieces with crayons. Michael lives near Chicago, Illinois. He grew up in a very large family and wouldn't have had it any other way. Michael hopes that the readers of the "Patrick McStup's Mixed-Up Family" stories will be thoroughly entertained and have many good laughs.

Made in the USA
Coppell, TX
12 December 2020